Best Friends AND BULLIES

An Inspiring Story about a Girl with Disabilities

CATHERINE CHATMON

Best Friends and Bullies

Book Edition ISBN-13: 978-1-937925-28-4

Scripture quotations from the King James Version of the Bible.

Cover Design - Megan Dillon - CreativeNinjaDesign.com

Publisher: Book Jolt
BookJolt.com
An Imprint of:
Publishers Solution, LLC

Printed in the United States of America

Dedication

This book is dedicated to my parents, Miriam and James (Bill) Chatmon who were my love and support until God called them home to Heaven and to my friend Ann who brought a little excitement into the life of an only child.

Most of all . . . Soli Deo Gloria

A Word From the Author

Best *Friends and Bullies* is based, in part, on my personal struggles. I was born with the disorder known as Neurofibromatosis (NF) 1, but at that time, little was known about it. As an infant, I had a malformed hip socket which required the wearing of a brace and corrective shoes. The tell-tale signs of the bumps, known as neurofibromas began to manifest themselves early on as did the café-au-lait spots. I also experienced problems with my back which was eventually determined to be a curve in several places, which caused mobility problems.

Early medical records hinted at mild spina bifida. It was determined that I also had hydrocephalus. My parents chose not to place a shunt in my head when I was young, fearing not only complications but also the unknown. Hydrocephalus would become an issue in my adult years and would require the placement of a shunt and subsequently its revision. Each case of NF is different apart from the classic signs of the disorder, and those who have it will experience various symptoms as well as varying levels of pain.

Because of my physical issues and gullibility, bullying was a frequent occurrence for me in my childhood. In those days, they mistakenly called it teasing, and the advice given was often to ignore it. Although what I experienced probably pales to what Corrie experiences in this story, nonetheless, it was a part of my experience.

During those years, the Lord graciously provided a safe place for me in the person of my friend, Ann. It is her friendship that is central to this story.

Best Friends and Bullies

No story comes to fruition without the input of others. I owe a debt of gratitude to a man who was my pastor during a difficult season of my life, Dr. Howard Wilburn. In those dark hours, he directed my attention to the Psalms, encouraging me and helping me to mine the nuggets of truth and encouragement found in the Word of God for myself.

Today the Children's Tumor Foundation (https://www.ctf.org/) is leading the charge on Neurofibromatosis research and information. Much of the material from Corrie's report can be verified at that site. Other parts are based on personal experience and medical records.

As the book states, the NF journey is different for each person who is placed on the NF Road. My NF journey is my own, and so are those journeys of fellow travelers.

I hope to be an encouragement to parents and to children who, by no choice of their own, have undertaken that same journey. By the grace of God, I desire to share my journey with you and to be an encouragement through the written word.

Soli Deo Gloria,

Catherine Lynn Chatmon, Ed.D.

Table of Contents

Chapter 1
Bad News–Good News

Corrie Cushman's mind seesawed between the math worksheet in front of her and her upcoming doctor's appointment. Her concentration was broken by a knock at the classroom door. As Mrs. Sharpe, her teacher, crossed the classroom to answer it, Corrie began gathering her belongings to leave. However, Mrs. Sharpe returned to the classroom, followed by a girl who looked around the classroom uncertainly.

Mrs. Sharpe stood at the front of the classroom and clapped once – her signal to the class to pay attention. A few students returned the signal by clapping twice. Mrs. Sharpe clapped again, and this time the entire class returned the signal promptly. She smiled at the class and at the girl standing next to her.

"Boys and girls," she said, "I want to welcome Lizzie Long to our class."

The class clapped again, welcoming Lizzie who smiled shyly at her new classmates.

When the clapping had died down, Mrs. Sharpe asked Corrie to stand and said, "Lizzie, this is Corrie. I'd like for you to sit in the desk behind her. Perhaps tomorrow, she can show you around the school during PE."

Best Friends and Bullies

Lizzie took the appointed seat as Corrie smiled gratefully at her teacher and thought, "I really like Mrs. Sharpe. It sure seems as though she is always thinking of ways to make me feel good about what I can do rather than always reminding me of what I can't do like other teachers I've had."

A quick look at the clock told Corrie that her mother would be there soon since it was almost time for her dreaded doctor's appointment. She quickly gathered her books and homework, then snapped the worksheet into her notebook, and deposited it and her spelling book into her backpack. Then she grabbed her library book to carry it out in her hand. Her number one rule was, "Never get into a car without a book to read."

A knock at the door interrupted her thoughts – just as Corrie suspected – it was her mother. Mrs. Sharpe nodded her approval for Corrie to leave. Corrie grabbed her belongings and joined her mother, and they walked to the car.

As they walked, Corrie asked her mother, "Now Mom, tell me again why am I seeing this ortho . . . ortho . . . oh, bone doctor?"

"Honey, do you remember what Dr. Robbins said when you had your physical?"

"She said my back was crooked and something about all those disgusting bumps and brown spots on my body."

"That's right. And remember we talked about how frustrated you get because you can't run as fast, or write as well as some of your classmates?"

"Yes, but why another doctor? I already saw Dr. Murphy," Corrie giggled at the thought. "He was so funny. He said I have neurotosis – is that right?"

Bad News - Good News

"Well, that's close. The word is neurofibromatosis. Most people simply call it NF."

"That's a lot easier to say, but you still haven't told me why I have to see another doctor."

"Dr. Murphy was concerned about your back. He wanted an orthopedist to look at it. So, he is sending you to Dr. Keener."

"And that's who I'm seeing today? Will he take any blood or give me shots?" Corrie asked worriedly.

"I don't think so," her mother replied. "Orthopedists don't usually give shots the first visit, and besides, your back problem probably isn't the kind that needs shots."

Corrie sighed with relief and climbed in the car with her mother. She fiddled with her backpack and finally opened her library book and began to read.

Her mother broke the silence, "Corrie, who is that girl that was sitting in the desk behind you? I thought you said that the desk was empty."

"It was, but a new girl moved here today. Her name is Lizzie; I am so excited because now I might have a friend in my grade. I wanted to hang out with her during afternoon recess, but instead, I have to come to this dumb doctor's appointment. Of all the days to get out early. Robin and Wendy will probably scoop her up to be in their group, and I'll be left out as usual. You know how they are . . ." Her voice trailed off.

"I know it hasn't been easy since Lori moved away, but someday you'll have that special friend," her mother spoke encouragingly.

Best Friends and Bullies

Corrie rolled her eyes but was prevented from speaking her mind, because they had just pulled up to the doctor's office. Making sure she had her book, she climbed out of the car and shut her door. She followed her mother into the doctor's office and sat down while her mother completed the registration process at the window.

As she rejoined her daughter, Mrs. Cushman remarked, "I do hope this doctor is on time. We need to hurry home and eat supper, and you need to finish your homework. We have that PTA meeting tonight."

Corrie moaned and asked, "Do I have to go? It will probably be soooo boring. Can't I just stay home and read?"

Mrs. Cushman smiled and shook her head, replying, "Daddy has to read the treasurer's report at the meeting, but remember afterward, the upper elementary Glee Club is singing. You were so disappointed because you missed them in assembly when you were sick. It won't be so bad."

Corrie was about to answer her mother when the nurse appeared at the door and called them back to see the doctor. She and her mother followed the nurse back to one of the examining rooms. Corrie was invited to have a seat on the bed while her mother took one of the chairs. She opened her book and continued to read. She was deeply involved in the mystery-solving abilities of her favorite sleuth. When the doctor opened the door, Corrie jumped and dropped her book. He stooped down and picked up her book and handed it to Corrie with a smile.

He held out his hand and said, "Hi, I'm Dr. Keener. You must be Corrie." Turning to the lady sitting on the chair, he said, "And you must be Corrie's mom."

Bad News - Good News

He looked at his clipboard and said, "I see that you have neurofibromatosis. What do you know about it?"

"I know I have brown spots on my body – my parents call them beauty spots. I have lumps – some of them hurt when people touch them. My handwriting is ugly, and I can't run and play as fast as other kids. I'm awful at running games and slow at math. My head is shaped in a weird way. One of the boys called me the girl with the stretched head. Sometimes my back hurts."

"Well, I would say you have a good grasp of your case of NF and how it affects you. Do you know what your spots and bumps are called?"

Corrie wrinkled her brow and said, "The lumps are neuro-something, and I just call the brown patches beauty spots like my parents do."

Dr. Keener smiled and said, "You're close on the lumps. They are called neurofibromas. Your brown spots are called café-au-lait spots. That means coffee with cream."

Corrie smiled and said, "That's what they look like – the coffee my mom drinks in the morning."

Dr. Keener said, "Corrie, there are several things I'd like to do today. First, I'd like to look at some of your café-au-lait spots and your neurofibromas. Second, I'd like for you to go through a series of movements for me. Third, I'd like to get some X-rays. Now, will you please lie back on the table, lift your shirt and let me feel some of your neurofibromas?"

Corrie frowned a little but complied with the doctor's request. She didn't like for people to see her body, but she reasoned that this man was a doctor and wanted to help. He could only help her if she let him do his job.

Best Friends and Bullies

Dr. Keener examined her skin very carefully. He poked and prodded a few of her bumps, asking from time to time, "Does this hurt?"

She usually answered, "No" or "Not much."

When he was finished examining her skin, Dr. Keener looked at her and said, "All right, Corrie, you've done very well. Now I want you to climb down and go through some movements for me."

Corrie slid off the table frowning, but she obeyed Dr. Keener. First, he asked her to hop on one foot and then the other. He told her to walk around the room, then bend over and touch her toes. She nearly fell when she attempted to bend over. Then he asked her to stretch her arms as high as she could. He asked her to pause at different times so that he could feel the movement of her muscles.

After observing her in different positions, Dr. Keener asked Corrie to sit on the table once again. He tapped her knees with a rubber mallet – to test her reflexes. As he laid the hammer down, he said, "Well, I do agree with Dr. Murphy that Corrie has NF. One last thing I'd like to do today is to take a series of X-rays because I think I detected a spine curve at several places. I also noticed some severe muscular weakness. A brace may help, but I'd like to see the X-rays first. Corrie, I'll step out of the room, and my nurse will come in and help you get ready."

In a few moments, the nurse knocked and entered with a robe and helped Corrie change into it. The nurse noticed the fear in her eyes. "This won't hurt a bit. All you have to do is lie still on a table and hold your breath when I tell you to."

Corrie nodded and followed the nurse to a big room with a hard gray metal table with a big machine hanging over it. She did just as the nurse told her and the X-rays were over quickly. They returned to the room where Corrie rejoined her mother. She slipped back into her own clothes and waited with her mother until a nurse came to escort her back to the waiting room. She tried to read the mystery book she had with her, but she was anxious about the results of those X-rays.

Meanwhile, Dr. Keener re-entered the room where her mother was waiting. He had the X-rays and a report in his hands. He sat down in a chair and began the conversation. "I have the results of the X-rays, but I also compared them with her earlier medical records. I noticed that she was diagnosed with mild spina bifida in infancy. I also noticed that she has hydrocephalus, but that you and your husband decided not to place a shunt in her head. I can sympathize with your decision in that area since she seems to be asymptomatic at this point. However, these X-rays confirm the fact that she does have curves of her spine. I think that a back brace may help offer support to her muscles. Here are some pamphlets describing it. I know you will want to talk to your husband and, of course, Corrie. I'll have them schedule a follow-up appointment for two weeks. That will give you time to discuss it."

Mrs. Cushman took the literature and said, "My husband and I need to review these, talk to Corrie, and, of course, pray about it. Thank you for your time."

She left the room and joined Corrie in the waiting room. Corrie was popping with questions but waited until the next appointment was made and she and her mom were in the car. "What did he say after I left? You know I hate it when doctors send me out of the room and then talk about me."

Best Friends and Bullies

"Well, he thinks that a brace may help strengthen your muscles. We need to talk to Daddy first, look at these pamphlets and, of course, we'll pray about it."

"I can tell you right now what I think God thinks about all of this . . . ," her voice trailed off at her mother's look of disapproval.

"We'll look at the pamphlets, talk, pray, and then we will decide." Corrie acquiesced with an "Okay," and resumed reading her book.

Because it was late, they stopped and picked up fried chicken and some sides for supper which were eaten quickly because the Cushman family had to be at the school early for Mr. Cushman's part in the PTA meeting – reading that boring financial report.

After endless reports and the Glee Club concert, Corrie and her mother were milling around in the crowd. A lady and a girl came rushing up to them. As they got closer, Corrie recognized the new girl who was in her class that afternoon.

When they got close enough to speak, the lady said to Mrs. Cushman, "Aren't you Jim Cushman's' wife? When he got up to give the treasurer's report, I said to myself, 'I know that man.'"

Mrs. Cushman replied, "I am, but I'm not sure I know you."

"I'm Margaret Long. We met at the home of a retired missionary couple several years ago."

"I'm Miriam Cushman, and this is my daughter, Corrie."

Mrs. Long said, "This is my daughter, Lizzie. She just started at Rivermont this afternoon. She's in Mrs. Sharpe's class."

The two mothers chatted for a while, while Corrie and Lizzie began to talk.

Bad News - Good News

Lizzie said, "I can't wait until our tour tomorrow. Be sure and show me everything, especially the library. It's my favorite place in the whole school. Can we eat lunch together, too? My mom usually packs my lunch."

Corrie responded, "I'll pack mine, too, and I can't wait to show you around – especially the library, because it's my favorite, too. Hey, let's find out if we can go to the refreshment table."

The girls obtained permission and made their way back to the table where they found some lemonade and cookies to munch on as they continued to talk. Soon it was time to leave.

As they left, Corrie said to her mother, "I'm glad we came tonight. And I'm glad we met the Longs. I hope Lizzie and I are going to be good friends. Maybe she won't like me when she finds out I can't run and jump very well. I'll bet she can do all those things."

Her mother replied softly, "I don't know, but take heart, Corrie, if Lizzie is a good friend, your physical problems and disabilities won't matter to her."

Corrie didn't say a word but silently continued to think mean thoughts about doctors, NF, and life in general.

Chapter Two

Corrie's Decision

When the Cushman family arrived home, they sat down to discuss the visit with the doctor. Mrs. Cushman spread the brochures out on the kitchen table.

Corrie picked one of them up and looked at it exclaiming, "Oh, it looks simply awful, and I'll bet it is dreadfully uncomfortable!"

Mr. Cushman chuckled, "Well, I have to agree with Corrie on both statements. I'm not sure I would want to wear something that looks like that. What do you think, dear?" he asked his wife. "You are the nurse in the family."

Mrs. Cushman replied, "Well, it can't hurt to try. Besides, I really think Dr. Keener really wants us to give it a chance."

"Humph!" Corrie said, "I wonder how much money he's making for every brace he talks people into buying?"

"Oh, Corrie, what a question!" said her dad laughing!

"She's your daughter, dear," responded Mrs. Cushman.

Mr. Cushman eyed his daughter with obvious affection and said, "I see a young lady who's about to fall asleep so let's continue this discussion tomorrow."

With those words, Corrie headed for her bedroom where she undressed and put on pajamas and climbed into bed.

Best Friends and Bullies

She sank beneath the covers and waited for her parents to come and tuck her in with goodnight kisses. Her last thoughts before she drifted off to sleep were in the form of a prayer, "Please, God, let them say I don't have to wear that old brace. Amen"

The next morning, Corrie crawled out of bed and felt her way to the bathroom. She sloshed some water on her face, ran a brush through her hair, threw a robe around her shoulders, and staggered to the kitchen.

"Good morning, Merry Sunshine," her mother said.

Corrie scowled as she said, "Good morning."

Her mother placed a bacon sandwich in front of her. "Here you go. I thought you'd like a special treat for breakfast this morning. What would you like to drink?"

"May I have some juice, please?"

"I think there is some grape juice, will that do?"

"That sounds good. Thank you."

After breakfast, Corrie rinsed her dishes and put them in the dishwasher. Then she went to her room to get ready for school. She was so glad it was warm; that meant she could wear capris, a cute top, and tennis shoes. Her mother put her hair in pigtails. She got her backpack and lunch, kissed her mom goodbye, and left for school.

The morning dragged by, especially since math class was first – all those numbers were so confusing. Literature class was a little better; they were reading *Charlotte's Web*. Their science and social studies lessons would be extensions of the story. It was interesting even if they did have to talk about and look at pictures of those yucky spiders. Finally, it was time for PE, and Corrie and Lizzie could begin their

Corrie's Decision

tour. They walked down to the kindergarten wing without saying a word. Then Corrie started to speak in her very best tour guide voice.

"Welcome to Rivermont Elementary School. You have just arrived in the kindergarten/first-grade wing. It is here that schooling has its beginning." With those words, both girls collapsed in a heap of giggles. They attempted to suppress their laughter lest a passing teacher hear them and reproved them for the excessive noise.

When Lizzie was able to speak again, she said, "Oh, Corrie, you are so funny. You crack me up."

The ice was broken, and the two girls concentrated on getting to know one another. They continued their conversation as Corrie pointed out the gymnasium, the cafeteria, and finally, the library.

As they walked into the library, Corrie remarked, "I've saved the best for last. This is my most favorite room in the whole school."

Mrs. Kegan, the librarian, walked over and greeted the girls, "Well, how's my bookworm today? Who's your friend?"

"I'm fine. This is Lizzie; she's a new girl in our class."

"Hello, Lizzie, it's nice to have you at Rivermont," Mrs. Kegan responded.

Then she turned to Corrie and said, "The mystery book you wanted has come in. I've been saving it for you. Come to the desk, and I'll sign it out to you."

Corrie retrieved her book and then joined Lizzie exploring the library. As the girls turned to go, Lizzie turned to Corrie and said, "Do you like to read mystery books, too?"

Best Friends and Bullies

Corrie replied enthusiastically, "Oh yes! I just finished a book about a girl whose family was in the witness protection program and she kept blowing their cover. When I saw you yesterday, I was sort of hoping your family was helping the FBI, but even if you were, I guess you couldn't tell me."

"Corrie, do you know something? You are crazy, but I just know we are going to be really great friends."

Lizzie continued their conversation, "Honestly, we're pretty boring; my daddy is a pastor. We've just decided to start a church in the basement of our house."

Corrie's eyes widened with wonder as she said, "Lizzie, that is so neat. It must be really cool to go to church in your house. At least you are never late for Sunday school."

"Yeah, but you can't think of a reason to skip, because you are always there. I remember being sick one Sunday, and Mom and Daddy gave me a yardstick and told me to beat on the wall if I needed them. That was really weird, but it worked. I just hope I don't get sick too much."

As they arrived at the classroom, Lizzie said to Corrie, "Thanks so much for showing me around. I hope you didn't mind not getting to play today."

"That's all right. I really don't enjoy PE very much anyway. I've never been very good at all those games. Besides, everybody laughs when I make a mistake."

The two girls walked into the classroom as the rest of the class was coming in noisily from PE. Mrs. Sharpe called them to order by clapping, and the children returned the clap. Then they began a spelling review game before lunchtime in the cafeteria.

Lizzie went through the line for milk and then joined Corrie, where they continued their conversation. Never

14

had lunchtime passed so quickly for Corrie, but as the girls left to walk back to the classroom, that nagging doubt crept in, "Would Lizzie really want to be my friend if she knew I might have to wear a brace on my back?"

When school was out, the girls waited in front of the school for Lizzie's mother, because they had promised Corrie a ride home even though she only lived three houses from the school. As she climbed out of the car, she turned and said, "Thanks for the ride. See you tomorrow." With those words, she turned and walked into the house where her mother was waiting for her.

After a snack, she worked on her homework while her mother prepared supper. After supper that evening, her parents brought out the dreaded pamphlets and spread them on the table. As they viewed the brochures, they realized again that there were no cures for NF; they also realized that the brace would not straighten Corrie's spine, but there was a possibility that it would strengthen her weakened muscles especially when coupled with physical therapy.

There was also the possibility that the brace would keep further curvature from occurring. Corrie was obviously not happy about any of it – it made her feel too different from her peers. Sensing her reluctance, her, parents agreed to delay any definite decision for a few days.

After reviewing her spelling words with her mom, Corrie took a bath and prepared for bed. She grabbed her book and crawled beneath the covers, eager to continue reading the book she had begun at the doctor's office. Corrie read until her mother came in to tuck her in and turn out the light. Having Lizzie as a friend made books with deep friendships enjoyable. Before she met Lizzie, she longed to have friendships like those described in the story and reading about the children and their adventures always made her feel a little sad and lonely. Now things looked like they were going to be different. With that, Corrie drifted into a deep sleep.

As Corrie was walking to school the next morning, she heard a honk from a car coming up behind her. She turned around and was pleasantly surprised to see Lizzie and her mother coming down the street. She gladly accepted the ride. The two girls chatted during the brief ride about the practice spelling test to be given that day. Any student receiving 100 percent on Wednesday would be given extra library time on Friday while the rest of the class took the regular spelling test. So far, Corrie had managed to earn her extra time unless she was absent or sick on Wednesday. The spelling test was given in the morning, and both girls made their desired 100's.

The first test of their friendship, however, was a little shakier. During PE, the girls in the class were given court time which gave them access to the hopscotch, four-square, and basketball courts in addition to a place where they could play jump rope. Lizzie and Corrie had decided to claim a hopscotch board on the court.

Before they began to play, Robin walked over and asked if she could join their game. Corrie didn't like the idea, but Lizzie really wanted Robin to join them so that she could meet other girls. Rather than explain her reluctance, Corrie agreed to Robin's joining their game. Robin was up first. She made it all the way to seven without missing.

Then Lizzie followed, making it just as far. Corrie, feeling the pressure of the goal she had to meet, stumbled and fell

Corrie's Decision

skinning both knees. She hadn't even made it off the first block. Lizzie immediately moved to help her up.

She asked, "Corrie, are you sure you are all right?"

With tears in her eyes, Corrie answered, "I think so, but my knees really hurt, and they're bleeding."

Lizzie replied, "Maybe you'd better go back to the classroom and let Mrs. Sharpe see." She attempted to take Corrie's arm, but a scowl from Robin made her stop.

Robin remarked within a smirking tone, "Corrie's so clumsy. Come on, Lizzie, let's finish our game and let the klutz go back to the teacher and get patched up. You still have one friend who has it all together." With those words, she struck a pose.

Lizzie eyed Corrie and said, "You can make it back to the classroom alone, can't you? I mean you can stand, and it doesn't look like anything is broken. No sense in both of us missing the game, is there?"

Corrie mumbled, "No, I guess not." With those words, she slowly and dejectedly made her way back to Mrs. Sharpe, who immediately sent her to the school nurse for first aid treatment.

The rest of the day passed slowly for Corrie, especially since Lizzie decided to eat with Robin, and she clearly wasn't invited. She could hardly wait to get home and lose herself in the world of her latest mystery book.

That evening, Corrie told her parents about the awful day. Then she added, "I'll wear the brace. I'll do anything that might make me less clumsy. At first, I was afraid that Lizzie wouldn't like me if I wore a brace, but now it doesn't matter. I don't think she likes me anyway. There's no telling what Robin said about me."

Best Friends and Bullies

It hurt Mr. and Mrs. Cushman to see their daughter so upset, but they also knew that things in relationships tended to work themselves out. Their discussion was interrupted by the loud ringing of the phone. Mr. Cushman rose to answer it.

He turned immediately to Corrie, and said, "Corrie, it's for you. It's Lizzie."

Corrie took the phone hesitantly.

"Corrie, it's me, Lizzie."

"Well, what's up?" Corrie answered guardedly.

"I'm calling to say, I'm sorry for leaving you on the playground when you got hurt. I am also sorry for letting you eat lunch alone. I told my parents what happened, and they said I was wrong to treat you like that."

"That's all right."

"You mean you aren't mad?"

"Well, I was at first, but I'm all right now. Lizzie, does this mean that we're still friends?"

"Oh, yes! Another thing that helped me to decide was the way Robin acted today. Do you know she never has a good thing to say about anyone? I really don't think she likes anybody."

Corrie giggled but kept her own opinion about Robin to herself. Before they hung up, Lizzie said, "I think my mom wants to talk to your mom. Can she come to the phone?"

"Sure," said Corrie. "I'll get her."

As Corrie heard one end of the conversation, she could tell that arrangements were being made for Lizzie to come over after school on Friday afternoon. It would really be a good day since it was library day as well. Mrs. Long and Lizzie would drop off a change of clothes for Lizzie and then take Corrie to school with them.

Suddenly Corrie was resolved to wear the brace and to tell Lizzie about it at the first opportunity. A real friend would understand.

Chapter 3

Corrie's Dilemma

Corrie dawdled over breakfast on Friday morning. Her determination to wear the brace had faded somewhat over the past two days. She was desperately afraid of what Lizzie would say, but even more, she was scared of Robin's scorn when she discovered that Corrie was even more different. Her mother sensed her distress and offered to call Robin's and Lizzie's mothers.

Corrie replied dejectedly, "Thanks, Mom, but they'd think I was a big baby and even bigger tattletale. Nobody would ever like me again . . . not that they do now."

Swallowing her last bite of toast, Corrie excused herself, went to the bathroom where she brushed her teeth and gave her bangs one last comb through. She grabbed her backpack and lunch, kissed her mother goodbye, and headed out the door. At that moment, Lizzie and her dad pulled into the driveway. Lizzie jumped out of the car and said, "Here are my clothes; if you take them into the house, I'll take your backpack and lunch."

Corrie replied, "Oh, that's right. Of course I'll take your clothes. I'll be right back."

Corrie hurried into the house and returned to the car. They rode the short distance to school without saying much because things were still a bit tense with them. Corrie did remember to say, "Thank you" to Lizzie's dad before she climbed out of the car.

As the girls walked into the school, Lizzie decided to break the ice.

"Aren't you glad that we don't have to take that spelling test today? We get to spend over an hour in the library."

"I know. That's one reason I love Fridays, but I'm anxious about next week. We have that big math test on Tuesday and a social studies test on Thursday. I hate Thursday tests because we have church on Wednesday nights."

"I know that makes it harder. Maybe we can start studying tonight. I am so scared about that math test. Numbers are so confusing."

"Really? You hate math, too? I never realized that there was someone else who hated math in our class. I'm so glad you're in our class, maybe we can help each other if we do it together."

They walked into the classroom and sat down. Mrs. Sharpe called the class to order. She reminded them of the spelling test they were going to have that morning. Then she asked those who had made 100 on the practice test to line up at the door. Lizzie, Corrie, Robin, and Ellen were then dismissed to go to the library.

However, before they left, Mrs. Sharpe reminded the class of a few things.

"Class, as you know, you have a book report due two weeks from today. Please select your books today if you haven't done so. Remember, the only requirement is that you read a book you have never read before. Many of you have gotten into a rut, and you need to try new things. Before you leave, are there any questions?"

Corrie's Dilemma

The class was silent, so she dismissed the four girls to go to the library, and the rest of the pupils began to take their spelling test. As the four girls made their way to the library, they quietly talked about the book report assignment.

Robin began venting, "I like the mystery book I'm reading. It's the tenth in the series and the third one I will have done a report on. I'll bet Mrs. Sharpe won't even notice unless the Goody Goodies with us tell her."

Ellen said, "Well, you know I won't tell." She turned to Lizzie and Corrie and said, "I guess you'll do what Mrs. Sharpe says, or you'll be afraid she won't like you."

Corrie shrank back, but she managed to say, "What's the big deal? I'd like to do the book I'm reading, but I think I'll try something new."

Lizzie agreed, "Me, too. Let's suggest books to each other. We're bound to have different ideas."

They stopped their conversation as they entered the library and began browsing the shelves. Corrie said, "Here's one, *Beezus and Ramona*. Ramona causes all kinds of trouble for her older sister. It's funny."

Lizzie replied, "Sounds fun, let me see it. Have you read the first book in this series, *The Boxcar Children*?"

"I've heard of it, but isn't that the book where the kids' parents are dead, and they run away from their grandfather? Books like that scare me."

"Corrie, you worry too much."

"I know, but I'm so afraid my parents are going to die."

"You really need to learn to trust God. Here's another one – *The Trumpet of the Swan*. I haven't read it, but it's by the same guy that wrote *Charlotte's Web* so it must be good. Let's sit down and read for a few minutes."

The girls took their books and sat down at a table and began reading. Soon the class joined them, and Mrs. Kegan led them in a game related to finding different books and pieces of information in the library.

After they returned to the classroom, they began attacking their various subject areas, including a review for their upcoming math test. Shortly after lunch, a messenger arrived from the other fourth-grade class. The note she bore said, "We the girls of Mrs. Foltz's class do hereby challenge the girls of Mrs. Sharpe's class to a kickball game next Monday."

Mrs. Sharpe read the note aloud and asked the girls to vote on whether or not they wanted to play. They voted unanimously to participate. The message was written out, and Ellen was chosen to carry it to the other class. Robin, who was the best kickball player in the class, raised her hand.

When she was recognized, she asked, "Can we pick the nine best players like they do in baseball? We'll never win with . . ."

Mrs. Sharpe cut her off before she could name any names saying, "That's enough, Robin. Our games are for everyone, and everyone will play."

Robin slumped down in her seat and muttered, "Oh great; We'll never win with clumsy Corrie and her fat friend." The stage whisper did not reach Mrs. Sharpe's ears, but Corrie and Lizzie heard it clearly and were reminded that they were both objects of Robin's scorn.

Corrie's eyes were about to fill with tears, but Lizzie quickly asked if the two of them could be excused, allowing

Corrie's Dilemma

them to escape to the restroom. Once there, Corrie leaned up against a sink and let the tears come.

Lizzie attempted to comfort her, saying, "Oh, come on Corrie, at least she didn't call you fat. She mainly says those things because she knows they upset you so much."

Corrie finally composed herself and returned to the classroom with Lizzie. The atmosphere was tense. Robin sat in her seat, looking like the cat that swallowed the canary. Mrs. Sharpe was trying to begin a discussion on Ponce de Leon and his quest for the Fountain of Youth.

Bobby spoke up from the back of the room, "That's crazy! Who would want to stay young forever? I mean, I can't do this; I can't go there. I can't go here. Rules! Rules! Rules! I can't wait until I'm grown and can do what I want."

Mrs. Sharpe answered, "I know how you feel, but growing up is no assurance that you'll be free from rules. I don't think you'll ever get to the point where you don't have to worry about them."

Lizzie raised her hand, and when she was recognized, she said, "Mrs. Sharpe, I have an idea. Why don't we ask our parents about the Fountain of Youth this weekend? Then on Monday we can write what they said about it and give our own opinions as well – you know if we'd drink from it and stuff like that."

Mrs. Sharpe responded, "Lizzie, that's a splendid idea. I think that will be your only homework this weekend besides reading your library books."

As they lined up, both Lizzie and Corrie heard Bobby mutter, "Leave it to a girl to think up more work for us to do."

The girls headed immediately for the ball diamond. Once there, they decided not to play in teams, but to cover

Best Friends and Bullies

the bases, have one pitcher and one girl in left and right field. The rest of the girls would remain in the infield. One girl would kick the ball when it was rolled to her and then run to first base. Once she reached home, everyone would rotate positions. The pitcher would then come to the infield. This would allow every girl to play every position during the practice sessions. All went well until Corrie was up to kick. Robin, who was pitching the ball, rolled it at such a blistering rate that Corrie went down as she ran and attempted to kick it. Lizzie was immediately at her side to help her up and to escort her to the classroom.

Robin called spitefully after her, "No fair! This messes everything up. Now I have to pitch longer, and I probably won't get a second turn to kick!"

Lizzie quickly responded, "Be quiet, Robin! You shouldn't have rolled it so hard. Besides, I never even got my first kick, and I started in the outfield."

Once they were in the classroom, and Mrs. Sharpe saw the reopened wounds, she sent the two girls immediately to the nurse. As they walked in, the nurse looked up from her desk and said, "I'll be with you in just a minute."

Corrie's eyes brimmed with tears, and she said shakily, "I know I shouldn't have tried it, but I'm so tired of being different from everybody else. I usually don't run well, and everybody laughs at me. I thought maybe things would be different today. I'm just a big klutz."

The nurse worked briskly to repair the damage. When Corrie was patched up to her satisfaction, she sent them back to class with the words, "I think you better skip the games during PE for the next few days. I'll send a note back to Mrs. Sharpe."

Corrie's Dilemma

"Oh, thank you for your help," Corrie replied. "I'll be sure to follow your directions."

The class was just coming in from playing when Corrie arrived back at the classroom. The rest of the afternoon sped by as the class engaged in various review games. Corrie was thinking that Mrs. Sharpe really knew how to make learning fun. Soon it was time for dismissal and the weekend that was ahead.

As the girls were walking home, Lizzie turned to Corrie and said, "All right, Corrie, what gives? You've fallen twice this week. That's more than I've fallen the past two months. I don't think you're doing it to get attention or to get out of anything, because you don't seem to be like that. I'm pretty sure both times were accidents. I don't want to be rude, but is there something wrong with you?"

Corrie looked at Lizzie in amazement, but she was desperately afraid to tell what needed to be said. Stalling for time, she said, "I'll tell you, but first let's go inside, change into our play clothes and have a snack. Then I promise I will tell you."

Later the girls were sitting in the swing in Corrie's backyard. Lizzie turned to her and said, "Now, will you please tell me what's going on with you?"

Corrie replied, "Okay, but first let's play a game. It's called would you like me if . . ."

Lizzie said, "I've never heard of it, but okay. How do you play it?"

"Well, we think of a horrible thing we could do or look like, and ask the other person, would you like me if? Here's one, would you like me if my hair turned purple and my skin turned orange?"

Best Friends and Bullies

"Corrie, that's crazy! Nothing like that is going to happen, but of course, I would like you. We're friends, and just because you might look weird, nothing would change the fact that we are friends."

"Now it's your turn."

"Okay, but I don't know what this has to do with anything. Would you like me if all my hair fell out and the top of my head turned hot pink?"

"Of course, as you said looks don't matter since we're friends. Okay, my turn again. Would you like me if something happened and I had to wear a brace, and I was even worse at running, playing games and other stuff?" At that point, Corrie began to cry.

Lizzie looked helpless for a minute and then she reached out to Corrie with her hand and said, "Of course, as I said, we're friends, but we're not playing anymore are we?"

Corrie shook her head, but just couldn't talk, and so Lizzie kept on talking, "You know Corrie, that really hurts my feelings. I know we don't know each other all that well, but you're a special friend to me. A brace isn't going to change things. I like you for who you are, not for what you can or can't do."

Corrie smiled with relief because she knew she had found a true friend. She was ready to tell Lizzie everything and to tell her mother that she could go ahead and call the doctor to schedule the needed appointments. She finally found the courage to wear the brace.

Chapter 4
An Adventurous Afternoon

Monday morning the doorbell rang just before 8:00. When Corrie answered the door, she was surprised to see Lizzie standing on the porch.

"Good morning, Corrie. Daddy had to make a call at the hospital. A lady in the church is having surgery this morning, so I figured we could walk to school together."

Corrie replied, "Sure, but I need to brush my teeth and grab my books."

In just a few minutes, Corrie emerged from her room, ready to face the day. She picked up her books and lunch from the hall table and called out, "Bye, Mom, we're leaving now."

Mrs. Cushman stepped out of the kitchen and said with a smile, "Not until you've kissed your mother goodbye."

Corrie planted a kiss on her mother's cheek while squeezing her hand three times – that was their secret code for "I love you."

As Corrie and Lizzie started their walk to school, Lizzie asked, "Did you remember to ask your parents about the Fountain of Youth?"

A look of dismay came over Corrie's face as she exclaimed, "Oh no! I completely forgot."

Best Friends and Bullies

Lizzie replied, "It will probably be all right. Mrs. Sharpe seems nice. Maybe she won't be too upset."

Corrie mumbled, "Maybe not, but I wouldn't count on it." Then changing the subject, she asked, "What did your parents think of the Fountain of Youth?"

"Well," Lizzie began, "Daddy thought that Ponce De Leon was trying to avoid dying rather than staying perpetually young. The churches back then didn't offer much hope. He thinks they were looking for Heaven on earth – you know everlasting life. But who would want to live forever here?"

"That is so cool! You will have a great report to write up, and I'll just sit there like a bump on a log."

"You know Mrs. Sharpe will never let you do that. She'll find something for you to do so that you don't waste time."

Corrie rolled her eyes and said, "Yeah, I figure she'll find something, but the question is, 'Will I want to do it?'"

The girls arrived at school and found their seats in the classroom. When the class was called to order, and all the break money was turned in, Mrs. Sharpe asked, "How many of you remembered to ask your parents about the Fountain of Youth?"

Corrie looked around in dismay as she noted that every hand was up. Even the kids who normally sloughed off on assignments appeared to have completed it. Mrs. Sharpe commended the class for their high level of participation and asked them to take out a sheet of paper and write about the responses they had gotten. Then she asked to see Corrie at her desk. Corrie took her time getting there, but instead of the scolding she expected, Mrs. Sharpe simply asked, "So did you forget about this one, Corrie?"

Corrie nodded her head too ashamed to speak.

An Adventurous Afternoon

Mrs. Sharpe simply said, "Why don't you write another kind of paper. Pretend you have found the Fountain of Youth. Would you drink from it? I know you really enjoy creative writing and you are quite good at it."

With a lighter heart, Corrie returned to her seat to begin the alternate assignment. After a few minutes, there was a knock at the door. The secretary from the office handed a note to Mrs. Sharpe.

Corrie looked up from her paper, where she was explaining her reasons for not drinking from the Fountain of Youth. Mrs. Sharpe beckoned to her to come to her desk again.

"Corrie, you have a doctor's appointment at 1:30 this afternoon. Your mom will pick you up. You won't miss anything except PE and science. I'll make sure you have a list of the homework assignments before you leave."

As she returned to her desk, Lizzie's eyes met hers. She nodded, which meant, "We'll talk later."

During the morning break, they got their chance. Corrie explained about her doctor's appointment. Lizzie's eyes lit up with delight, "Corrie, do you know what this means?"

"Yeah, I'm getting the brace."

"No, it means you miss the kickball game. You don't have to sit on the bench and just watch."

Corrie was elated and excitedly said, "And I don't have to listen to Robin's remarks."

Later that afternoon, Corrie sat in the doctor's waiting room with her mother again. When the nurse called her, Corrie and her mother rose to follow her. She led them to an examining room and said, "Please remove your outer clothes so I can measure you for the brace."

Corrie looked at her mother and asked with her eyes, "Must I?"

Best Friends and Bullies

Her mother gave her a gentle nudge and said, "Go ahead, dear. It's the only way we can be sure the brace will fit."

The nurse said tenderly, "Aw, go on, honey! There's nobody here but us girls."

Once the measurements were taken, Corrie was allowed to put her clothes back on before further instructions were given. Then the nurse said, "The brace will be ready in three to five days. It would be good if you had some clothes that were slightly larger to accommodate the brace. Do you have any questions?"

Corrie shook her head but remembered to thank the nurse. She remained silent as her mother scheduled the next appointment. Her silence continued as they got into the car, but the look in her eyes warned her mother that it was probably the calm before the storm. They got into the car, and Corrie exploded, "Oh, Mom, this is terrible. With bigger clothes and that brace, I'll look simply awful. Everyone will laugh and stare at me. What am I going to do?"

Her mother responded, "You could never look awful, and it won't matter to your real friends."

Corrie replied, "It's not my friends I'm worried about . . . It's people like Robin. I can just hear her now. She already calls me, Clumsy Corrie."

Her mother said, "I know, dear, but we all have our Robins to deal with. It may be good that you're learning while you're young. If it gets too bad, you can always talk to Mrs. Sharpe."

"Okay, but only if it gets too bad."

"Corrie, there's one other thing I have to tell you. I have to work tomorrow. I've asked the Longs if you could go home with Lizzie, so Mr. Long will pick both of you up at school."

An Adventurous Afternoon

"Cool! Maybe I can forget that dumb brace for a few hours."

The next afternoon, Corrie and Lizzie waited at the car pick up for Mr. Long to get them. When they arrived home, they quickly changed into play clothes and then had a snack. Afterward, they went out into the backyard to explore. There wasn't much grass; just a lot of dirt and lots of trees. There was a hammock tied between two strong trees, but the neatest thing was a creek way down in the backyard.

Seeing the creek, Corrie asked, "Hey, Lizzie, can we wade in the creek? It's so warm today?"

"No, we'll have to wait until it's warmer."

"What if we accidentally fall in?"

"That won't work; I tried it yesterday. Mom said if I tried it again, I would be in big trouble. I think that means a scolding, but I don't want to find out."

"That reminds me of something that happened to Daddy when he was a little boy. There was a creek near his house that he passed every day on his way home from school. I think it was called Tar Branch. One day, it was a little cool, so he went wading with his shoes on. When he didn't get home from school on time, my grandpa came looking for him and caught him wading in the creek. Grandpa told him he was going to get punished for ruining his shoes and that the next time he wanted to wade in the creek, he should remove his shoes. Well, my dad waited until December and went wading in the creek again. He took his shoes off and put them on a big rock. This time grandpa came down all ready to punish him again. I mean, shouldn't he know not to wade in the creek when it's freezing cold? But my daddy said, 'But Dad, you said you wouldn't punish me if I just took my shoes off.' So, he got by with it. He's was a quick thinker. "

Best Friends and Bullies

"That's hilarious, but we still better not try it. Come on up to the dog house. I want you to meet my dog. He's a Dalmatian; so, we call him Dall or Dally."

Dall was a beautiful Dalmatian – he had the cutest baby blue eyes, and he looked like he was tan with brown spots. When Corrie remarked about his unusual coloring, Lizzie laughed and replied, "He does look different. He's really black and white, but he looks tan and brown because he rolls around in the dirt. It's his favorite thing to do."

Corrie stood back because she had bad experiences with big dogs. Lizzie said, "Aw come on, Corrie, he won't hurt you. Let me introduce the two of you."

Then she turned to Dall and said, "Sit, Dally. Now shake hands with Corrie."

To Corrie's amazement, he extended his right paw. She hesitantly took it.

Then she said, "Oh, Lizzie, you are right. He is a sweet dog. He's not like other big dogs I have known."

Lizzie turned to Corrie and said, "I have an idea what we could play. Remember that story we read a couple of days ago about the hikers in the Alps and how the rescue dogs came out to find them? Let's pretend that we are lost in the Alps and that Dall is the rescue dog who comes to find us. I can go into the house and get some cookies and put them in a bag and tie them to Dall's collar. I'm not sure what we can do for a drink. I guess we'll just get a plastic cup and pretend."

Lizzie ran inside and got the things they would need for the game. She put the cookies in a paper sack along with the plastic cup and then tied it shut with string. She told Corrie to go hide behind one of the trees while she released Dall. However, he wanted nothing to do with their game. Instead of playing rescuer, he pawed the paper bag loose, tore it open, and gobbled the cookies. He wasn't sure what to do with the cup, so he batted it around the yard. Corrie and Lizzie convulsed with laughter. It didn't matter that Dall had ruined their game. It just felt good to laugh together.

As they went inside, Lizzie remarked, "I guess you can't make a Saint Bernard out of a Dalmatian."

Laughing, they told Mrs. Long what they did, but she shook her head as she laughed and said, "Girls, girls."

Since their game was ruined, the girls decided to stay inside and study for a fractions test. After an hour of reviewing and devising problems, the girls were satisfied with their grip on the subject. So, they began reading their book report books. Each girl determined to have a final review of the fractions with their mothers before going to bed.

Mrs. Cushman came to get Corrie shortly after they started reading. She thanked Mrs. Long for allowing Corrie to stay the afternoon and then asked if the same arrangements could be made for the following afternoon. Much to the delight of the two girls, she agreed.

Lizzie got a gleam in her eye and asked, "Do you think we could walk home? It's not far, and there are policemen at the busiest streets. We'll be careful."

Mrs. Cushman got a look of concern on her face, and said, "Well, I don't know . . ."

Mrs. Long responded, "Oh, I think it will be fine. Lizzie has walked home several times. And there are policemen at the busiest streets."

Mrs. Cushman hesitated, "I'm just afraid Corrie will get too tired."

Best Friends and Bullies

Lizzie interjected, "Oh, we can stop to rest along the way. We'll be fine. Right, Corrie?"

Corrie reluctantly agreed, "If you think so."

So, it was settled. The girls would walk home together the following day.

The next day seemed to drag by. There was that dreaded fractions test. Both girls felt good about their performance on it, but they knew Mrs. Sharpe had to grade them, and it seemed she always found a mistake or two.

Finally, school was out. The only thing the girls had to do for homework was to complete an assignment in their spelling books and continue reading their book report books.

When they arrived, they noticed that the car was gone. Lizzie went to the secret hiding place, retrieved the key, and unlocked the door. Then she dropped the key in her pocket. Once they were in, they scouted around for a note explaining the whereabouts of Lizzie's parents. Sure enough, there was a note taped to the refrigerator which said, "Girls, we made a run to the office supply store. We are also stopping by the hospital because Mrs. Evans had emergency surgery. We plan to be home between 3:00 and 3:30. Help yourselves to a snack. LOCK THE DOOR!!!"

Lizzie found some chocolate chip cookies and Kool-Aid for them, which they ate as they began to look over their spelling homework. However, they discovered, to their dismay, that they had each written down a different section for their homework assignment. Corrie thought that Alex, who lived next door to her and was in their class, might have written it down correctly. She had called him at other times to get assignments when she had been absent from school. She was going to the phone but suddenly stopped. Both girls heard footsteps on the porch.

An Adventurous Afternoon

Corrie turned to Lizzie and said in a quiet whisper, "The door, did you lock the door?"

Lizzie gestured toward the door which was locked. At that point, there was a knock at the door. Both girls had been instructed never to open the door unless they were expecting someone, and Lizzie knew that her parents had house keys. She shook her head slightly and moved closer to Corrie. Another knock sounded, and Corrie opened her mouth to scream, but Lizzie immediately clapped her hand over her mouth to silence her.

She then whispered, "Come on, Corrie. We've got to get out of here. We'll slip out through the basement."

The girls tiptoed to the door leading to the basement. Corrie quietly opened the door and began descending the staircase. Lizzie followed then closed and locked the door. Once they were in the basement, Lizzie led Corrie to the outside door, but before they could exit, Corrie caught a glimpse of a shadow and heard Dall barking for all he was worth. They quickly retreated into the middle of the basement and huddled together in a corner away from the window. Dall finally stopped barking, but they remained there for what seemed like hours.

Finally, they heard footsteps upstairs, and Mr. Long calling, "Girls, where are you?"

Only then did the girls leave their hiding place and make their way upstairs. As they came through the door, Mr. Long asked, "Why were you in the basement?"

Lizzie replied, "We thought we heard something, so we locked ourselves in the basement."

Before they could say anything further, they heard a siren, and a saw a car with a blue light whiz by. Mr. Long looked at the girls and asked, "Lizzie, Corrie, exactly what did happen while we were gone?"

Lizzie answered, "We heard someone knock at the door. They kept knocking. We knew it wasn't you because you have a key. Dally was barking and everything. We were terrified; so, we hid in the basement and just waited for you to come home. We were so scared," she finished with a tear in her voice.

Her father put his arm around her and said, "You did the right thing, but did you think to pray? God cares about everything in your life. He was certainly looking after you today."

Corrie listened to him and wanted to ask if he really believed what he said about God. She wanted to ask if he thought God cared about NF and braces. She decided against it because God was obviously too busy protecting people and houses from prowlers. He was probably like a policeman watching and waiting for someone to mess up. That took so much time that He couldn't get it all done. No, she knew without asking that there was no sense bothering God about her brace. After all, she had prayed that the bumps would go away, but it seemed like she found a new one every day. She was sure that God was far too busy to bother with Corrie Cushman and NF.

Chapter 5
Corrie's Brace

As Corrie was eating breakfast on Thursday, her mother said, "Don't forget I'm picking you up right after school. Your brace is ready today."

Corrie's face fell, but then she got a gleam in her eye and asked, "Mom do you think Lizzie could come? It would really be nice to have a friend to go with us."

Her mother replied, "I think that would be fine. I'll ask Mrs. Long when they drop Lizzie off to walk to school with you."

When the Longs got there, arrangements were made for Lizzie to go with Corrie and her mother. As the girls walked to school, Lizzie said, "I'm so glad I get to go with you to get the brace; that way, I can be the first to see it."

"Lizzie, you act like you're enjoying this."

"Oh, Corrie, don't be so sensitive. I just want to help you get through this."

Later that afternoon, Corrie, her mother, and Lizzie sat in the waiting room. Both girls tried to read their books since their oral book reports were due soon. Finally, Corrie's name was called, and she and her mother followed the nurse back into a private room. Corrie's eyes got bigger and bigger as the nurse explained the procedure for wearing the brace. The nurse left the room to get the brace. When she came back to the room with it, Corrie burst into tears.

"Oh, Mom, look at it. It's so ugly. I just know it will be the most uncomfortable thing I have ever worn – even worse than that thing I wore when I was a baby."

The nurse helped her put it on and fastened it around her stomach. Soon Corrie was in the brace, and then she put her clothes back on. The nurse asked her to move in a variety of positions – bending over, reaching up, squatting, and finally sitting down. At that point, Corrie erupted again, "This thing is so uncomfortable. It's so heavy, and it presses on my legs when I sit down. I hate it!"

Mrs. Cushman looked at her daughter in sympathy, but addressed the nurse who was helping them, "Is there anything we can do to make it a little more comfortable?"

She replied, "It will be uncomfortable for a while, but you can put gauze pads at the tops of her thighs until she breaks it in."

Corrie caught a glimpse of herself in the mirror and began to cry again, "Oh, Mom, I really do look fat. What will Lizzie say; what will the other kids say?"

Her mother replied, "It won't matter to your real friends."

Corrie was about to roll her eyes but stopped herself— she knew her mother thought that was disrespectful, but she did eek out the words, "You always say that."

As they stepped back into the waiting room, Lizzie came running over to her and looked at her carefully, and said, "It really doesn't look bad. It's just a little lumpy. What does it feel like? Is it dreadful?"

Corrie exploded, "Lizzie, it's far worse than I ever expected. It has two padded bars in the back. It fastens in the front, and it's heavy and presses on my legs when I sit down. It's simply awful!"

Lizzie responded softly, "I know it must be simply awful, but I have an idea. Why don't you give it a name to make it seem more like a friend? You have named everything – all your stuffed animals and even that green ball."

Corrie replied, "I've already given him a name. It's Goofball because he's goofing up my life."

Lizzie and Mrs. Cushman looked at each other and suppressed a giggle. Fortunately, Corrie did not notice. The three of them made their way to the car. As they got in, Mrs. Cushman asked, "What do you say to pizza?"

Corrie perked up and said, "You mean at Ronzi's?"

Her mother nodded, and Lizzie asked, "What's Ronzi's?"

Corrie responded, "It's a really cool restaurant that serves the best pizza. Mr. Conelli owns it, and he is so friendly and funny. He tells the best jokes."

The three of them entered the restaurant where Mr. Conelli immediately greeted them, "Hey there, Corrie, how's my favorite pizza eater?"

Corrie returned the greeting, but simply mumbled, "Okay, I guess."

Mr. Conelli said, "Well now, you don't sound too sure about that, but I'll bet it's nothing that a slice of my pepperoni pizza won't cure. Say there, aren't you going to introduce me to your friend?"

Corrie's face blushed as she considered that her negligence might be interpreted as rudeness. She turned to Lizzie and said with a flourish, "Mr. Conelli, I want you to meet my friend, Lizzie. You know what? I don't think she has ever had pizza in a restaurant in her whole life."

Mr. Conelli laughed and said, "Well, we'll have to fix that, won't we? I just happen to make the best pizza you will ever eat."

Both girls laughed as he began his pizza-making theatrics. First, he grabbed some pizza dough and flopped it around on his wooden cooking counter. Then he tossed it in the air and caught it deftly. Then he pressed it into a pan and spread the marinara sauce all over it and topped it with cheese and pepperoni. Then he put it in his pizza oven. While they waited for the pizza to cook, he entertained them with a variety of jokes and other funny stories. When the timer dinged, he removed the pizza from the oven, cut it in eight even pieces, and set it before them.

Corrie offered Lizzie the first piece and then took one for herself. She closed her eyes and smiled as she took her first bite. When the last crumb had been devoured and the last drop of soda consumed, the girls thanked Mr. Conelli for making the pizza and Mrs. Cushman for treating them. On the way to the car, Lizzie confided to Corrie that this really was the first pizza that she had ever had in a restaurant and that it was more amazing than she could ever have imagined.

When Corrie and her mother dropped Lizzie off at her house, she hugged Corrie and whispered, "Don't worry about tomorrow. I will help you all I can."

The next morning Corrie dressed carefully to hide the despised brace as best she could. She was relieved when no one seemed to notice it. In fact, the day went well until it was time for PE. Tired of being on the sidelines, Corrie

Corrie's Brace

joined in the kickball game, despite Lizzie's questioning look. They quickly chose teams, and as usual, Corrie was picked last. When it came time for her to kick, Robin was pitching and rolled the ball at a blistering speed. As Corrie ran out to give it her hardest kick, her feet flew out from under her, and she landed on her back with her feet up the air. Her shirt caught on the brace, causing it to be revealed. Lizzie ran over to help her up and brushed the dirt off. Then she walked with her back to the classroom.

Mrs. Sharpe looked at Corrie and said, "You don't look seriously injured, but I'd feel better if Mrs. Evans had a look at you. Corrie, what were you thinking? You shouldn't have been playing at all."

Tears formed in Corrie's eyes as she made her way to the nurse's office. She knew that she had no business playing, but she was so tired of being different. She was always on the sidelines – watching. If she could just feel as though she belonged for once. If she could just silence the snickers and unkind words that were hurled her way. She wiped her eyes with the back of her hand just as she knocked on the door to Mrs. Evans' office.

Meanwhile, back in the classroom, Mrs. Sharpe and Lizzie had their own conversation. Lizzie prefaced her words by saying, "Mrs. Sharpe, I need to tell you something. I feel like a tattletale, but you really need to know this. Corrie just got a brace for her back. You know she has trouble walking and running. It's because of some condition she's had since she was baby, but I think this brace is going to make it a lot harder for her. Her mom wanted to send a note, but Corrie wouldn't let her. She's just tired of being different."

Mrs. Sharpe replied. "Thank you for telling me. I was aware of some of this, but I didn't realize that she had already gotten the brace. I think we will have to come up with a different plan for her for PE. Would you be willing to hang out with her? That way she won't feel so conspicuous. I can think of several ball-related games the two of you can play."

Lizzie's eyes shone as she replied enthusiastically, "Oh yes. That will be so much fun. I'm not very good at those games either." Then she added worriedly, "You won't tell anyone we talked and that you know about the brace?"

Mrs. Sharpe replied, "Never!"

The class came in from playing about that time and found their seats. Corrie returned from the nurse's office as well, looking none too happy. Lizzie raised her eyebrows, but Corrie shook her head and mouthed, "Later."

Mrs. Sharpe instructed the class to take out their book report books and read until lunchtime. She also asked for volunteers to begin presenting their oral reports the following day. Since she only had a few pages to go and a perfect idea about what she wanted to say, Corrie volunteered. Bobby also volunteered. Then for the next 20 minutes, there was silence in the room as the class read. Corrie finished her book and took out a sheet of paper and began to write. She had planned to do a grab bag book report – a book report using objects to highlight key events. She also knew that she would finish her book report without giving away the ending because she hoped others would be interested in reading the book.

After school, Lizzie and Corrie walked to Corrie's house where Mrs. Long would pick Lizzie up. On the way home, Corrie explained that when she went to the nurse's office, the nurse had really scolded her for attempting to play kickball. The nurse sent a note to Mrs. Sharpe recommending

Corrie's Brace

that Corrie be given alternative activities while the rest of the class engaged in PE—especially kickball games.

As soon as they arrived at Corrie's, Corrie went to her room and dropped her backpack in her room. She stopped to wash her hands and then went to the kitchen to see what sort of snack she could wrangle out of her mother. As she passed the spare bedroom, she was startled by a ferocious roar. Corrie screamed and dashed to the kitchen, where her mother was beginning to prepare the evening meal.

Corrie sought words to describe what happened. "Oh, Mom! I just know that there is a monster in the spare room. It's probably purple with green hair and huge teeth. It had such a loud roar! I am so scared!"

Her mother stopped what she was doing and hugged her daughter and said, "Corrie, you are just scaring yourself. You know there are no monsters. We went through that when you were five or six. Now, how about some cookies and juice for a snack?"

Before Corrie could answer, Lizzie appeared laughing and said, "That sounds great, Mrs. Cushman."

Mrs. Cushman whirled around and said, "Lizzie, where did you come from?" Then, turning to Corrie, she said, "There, my dear, is your monster."

Lizzie turned to Corrie grinning as she said, "I'm sorry, but I just love playing jokes on people."

"It's all right, but watch out, I'll get you yet, and maybe next time I'll be expecting it."

"Don't count on it,"

The girls laughed and took their snacks and went out to the carport. They were enjoying a leisurely time when Mrs.

Best Friends and Bullies

Long pulled up. Lizzie ran to pick up her books and joined her mother. The girls said their goodbyes and Lizzie left with her mother. Corrie retrieved her book and a note pad from the house. She sat in the giant swing in the backyard as she finished making notes for her book report. That evening her mother helped her get everything together and put the needed items in a bag for her grab bag book report.

The next afternoon, Corrie stood before the class and gave her report. She had her bag of items with her. After introducing her book, she reached into her bag and brought out a pair of binoculars. She told of Sam Beaver and his interest in nature. Then she pulled out a picture of a family of swans, explaining that baby swans were called cygnets. Then she told of the birth of Louis and his siblings. Next, she took out a small cassette player and played a few feet of blank tape, which she said reminded them that Louis was born with a handicap – he was born without a voice. Then she pulled out a toy trumpet and told of Louis' father's daring raid on the instrument store and about his stealing a trumpet to give his son a voice. She ended with the words, "Will the trumpet have the desired effect for Louis? What will happen because his father stole the trumpet? What about Sam Beaver, the boy who loves nature, what will happen to him? To get the answers to these questions, you need to read, *The Trumpet of the Swan* by E.B. White." The class applauded, and Corrie sat down, satisfied that she had done an excellent job.

She barely heard the next classmate's book report but knew he was sharing a funny book. Corrie was lost in her own thoughts, wondering if old Goofball was anything like Louis' trumpet. If so, perhaps there was hope for a normal

Corrie's Brace

life for her. As they went to lunch, Lizzie said to her, "When you take that book back to the library, I want it."

Corrie nodded as a happy feeling engulfed her. If there was anything better than reading a good book, it was sharing that good book with a good friend.

Chapter 6

Lizzie's Moving

The last week of school finally arrived. Lizzie and Corrie were excited not only about the closing of school, but because they had special plans for Thursday night – an end of school celebration. Lizzie had invited Corrie to spend the night, and Corrie was beside herself with excitement. It would be the first time she had spent the night with anyone outside of her own family.

Tuesday evening, the Cushman family was eating a leisurely dinner. Corrie could tell her parents were pre-occupied because much of the banter that they usually exchanged during the evening meal was missing.

As they were eating dessert, Mr. Cushman broached the subject that had been hanging over them, "Corrie, how would you feel about your mom returning to work full time?"

"You mean she would be working more than she is now?"

"Yes, there is a full time opening at the medical department at my company where she has been working part-time."

"Well, I guess it would be okay, but who would stay with me? I can't stay by myself, can I?"

"To be honest, we haven't thought that far ahead yet. We just wondered how you would feel about your mom's taking the job."

"If that's what she wants, I guess it's all right, but hey, I have an idea! Lizzie could come over and babysit me."

Best Friends and Bullies

At this point, Mrs. Cushman interjected a comment, "Oh, no! I can just imagine what my house would look like after the two of you had been home alone all day. Besides, I'm pretty sure there are laws against children staying alone."

"Yeah, but what fun!"

"Fun for whom?" her Dad asked. Then he added, "We don't have to decide anything tonight. Let's just think and pray about it for a couple of days, but let's not discuss it outside of the family just yet."

"You mean I can't tell Lizzie when we spend the night together Thursday night?"

"Exactly, that's what I mean."

Thursday morning as they walked to school, Corrie and Lizzie discussed their plans for their evening together. They were excited that they could play outside until dark since school was finally out. Lizzie's parents had planned to pick up both girls after school at the Cushman's house. Mrs. Cushman had intended to show Mrs. Long how to help Corrie with her brace. Then Corrie would go home with them for the evening and for the entire next day.

That evening as they sat around the supper table enjoying the spaghetti that Mrs. Long had prepared, Lizzie looked at her plate and broke into song, "Worms are greasy, slide down easy; I'm going out and eat worms."

Corrie's mouth was full of spaghetti, but she still began to giggle at Lizzie's antics and began to choke as a result. Mrs. Long made her raise her hands and gave several sharp whacks between her shoulder blades. It did the trick, and Corrie quickly recovered. She silenced Lizzie from further singing with a piercing look, but the gleam in Lizzie's eyes told her that she would be hearing more of the song when they were alone. After supper, the girls cleared the table and took care of the dishes. Then they went out to the screened-in porch where Lizzie introduced the subject of worms again.

"Now, Corrie, I want you to hear all the words, 'Nobody likes me. Everybody hates me, I'm going out and eat worms. Worms are greasy, slide down easy. I'm going out and eat worms. Little worms, big worms, chewy ooey gooey worms. I'm going out and eat worms.'"

"Lizzie, that's disgusting. I'm pretty sure it's what Mrs. Sharpe called a metaphor, and it describes someone who is really sad, but it's a really gross song. Where did you learn it anyway?"

"My older sister sings it to me when I'm pouting. It's supposed to make me laugh."

"Well, it makes me want to throw up. Eating worms? Yuck!"

"Corrie, I've got a great idea. Let's go out and dig for worms down at the creek."

Corrie wrinkled her nose and said as politely as she could, "Lizzie, I don't think that's a great idea. We don't want to disrupt the worm families. Besides what would we do once we captured them?"

"Corrie, you think too much. I really don't think worms have families. Besides, Mr. Lemley might buy them from us for five cents a worm. He goes fishing a lot and uses worms for bait. Last week Mr. Lemley asked if he could dig for worms at our creek. He also said if I ever wanted to make some money, I could dig worms for him. Look, he's out in the yard; I'll go ask him if he wants any this evening."

Best Friends and Bullies

Lizzie ran across the street where her neighbor was working in the yard and returned panting, but smiling. Between gasps for breath, she gave the news, "He says he wants all the worms we can dig, and he'll pay us a penny for each worm we can dig up." Lizzie ran and got her mother's garden spade and two tin cans. She was a tremendously fearless worm hunter. She could dig them out from anywhere. Corrie had been relegated to sit on a large stone where she was the designated keeper of the worms – in tin cans for she had adamantly declared, "I will not touch those things."

As she was sitting there on the rock, she took a few moments to drink in the summer evening. A pleasant cool breeze blew as the setting sun shed its last few rays before retiring for the night. The bobwhites were bidding goodnight to each other by name. The sky was brilliant with the colors peculiar to a summer sunset: bright blue with splotches of orange, red, and purple. A few dark threatening clouds dotted the sky. The sun was a glowing red ball about to be tossed over the western horizon only to return the following morning bouncing vibrantly in the east. It was a perfect evening.

When Mrs. Long called them at 8:30, they had captured fifty worms. Lizzie took them over to Mr. Lemley and returned with fifty cents. That wasn't bad for having fun."

After a bath, both girls were in Lizzie's room, getting ready to get into bed for a long talk. A look outside revealed that the bright sky had turned angry. Mrs. Long came into the room and told the girls that storm warnings had been reported on the radio. So far, they were only expecting severe storms in their area, but areas south of them were under a tornado watch. If anything changed during the night, they would have to move to the basement. Both girls fell into an uneasy sleep after Corrie called her parents just to hear their voices.

The night brought the storms and torrential rains, but nothing more. The morning brought the sun. Corrie was left with a sense of fear and dread leading to many, "what ifs?" She woke up before Lizzie did the next morning, dressed quietly, grabbed a book, and slipped out to the porch where she began to read. She figured that Mrs. Long could help her with the brace later on. She was deeply engrossed in her book when Lizzie snuck up on her and shouted, "Boo!"

Corrie jumped and screamed. Lizzie laughed, but Corrie couldn't understand why Lizzie enjoyed teasing her like that. She knew Lizzie wasn't trying to be mean; she just wished she could be as quick. Once again, she vowed to herself, "Someday I'll get her first."

Lizzie said, "Thank you for being so quiet this morning. I made your bed for you; I wanted to be nice to you as a guest. Mom is ready to help you with Goofball if you go back to the bedroom." Corrie complied and soon joined Lizzie for breakfast.

Over a breakfast of toast and jelly, the girls discussed their plans for the day. They had planned to walk to the Community Drug Store and Snack Shoppe to have lunch. They had the neatest soda fountain there. Mr. Cushman had provided fifty cents for each girl, and with the fifty cents from Mr. Lemley, there would be enough to have hot dogs, cherry colas, and ice cream. Corrie was beyond excited about this prospect. All the kids in her neighborhood, even the youngest, walked to the drug store. They were always talking about the fun they had. She had never been allowed to accompany them. She walked slowly because of the NF, and sometimes the kids liked to tease her in cruel ways. She and her mother imagined they might leave her alone in a store or by herself on the street corner because they liked to scare her. Because Lizzie's house was much closer to the Shoppe than Corrie's was, she had gotten permission to walk there with Lizzie. It was less than three blocks and even shorter if they went the back way.

Shortly before lunch, the girls set out on their excursion. When they arrived at the store, they seated themselves on the tall bar stools and ordered hot dogs and cherry colas. While waiting for their order, they spun around until they were both giggling and dizzy. After they had eaten their food topped off with hand-dipped chocolate chip ice cream, they climbed down from their stools. Mr. Bronson, the owner of the store, kept a plentiful supply of kid-friendly comic books. He never minded free-readers as he called the kids who wanted to sit on the floor beside the rack and read them. As soon as the girls finished reading the comics, they left the store remembering to say thank you for the great food and service.

As they made their way home, Lizzie turned to Corrie saying, "Corrie, I have good news and bad news for you. Which one do you want to hear first? "

"Definitely, the bad"

"Good, I was hoping you would say that."

"You seem awfully happy to be giving bad news."

"Well, I should have said good news, bad news, good news."

"Will you get on with it?"

"Lizzie went on to explain, "A new highway is being built. It's supposed to go smack dab through our house. We've been looking for and praying for a new house ever since we got the news. We have also wanted to have a building for our church. Well, we found a church building. The people who are meeting there want to move to a different community. Actually, we found it a while back, but Daddy said that we had to negotiate the price. Yesterday, he and two of the men from the church met and signed the papers. Corrie, we have a church! Now we can do some of the things we wanted to do, but we never had the room."

"That's cool! Well, I guess I'd better hear the bad news."

"The bad news is since we have to buy the parsonage with the church, Mom, Daddy, and I are moving to a new neighborhood. We had hoped to find something in this neighborhood, but we couldn't."

Corrie's face clouded over, and tears welled up in her eyes. She was going to have to say goodbye to another friend.

Lizzie interrupted, "Wait! Remember I told you there was good news, bad news, good news! Don't you want to hear the rest of it?"

Corrie merely nodded, and so Lizzie continued, "The rest of the good news is that our house is only three miles away, and I can still go to Rivermont."

Corrie stopped in her tracks, put her hands on her hips, and exclaimed, "Lizzie, you are a rat! You scared me half to death!"

Giggling, Lizzie pointed to Corrie and said, "Gotcha!"

Arms linked, they returned to Lizzie's house. Tired from their excursion, they got their books and settled down on the porch to read. They were so engrossed in their books when Dall's barking startled them. They looked up and saw Mrs. Cushman driving in. As soon as she got to the door, Corrie ran to her, yelling, "Guess what? Lizzie's moving!" Then she ran to get her overnight bag.

Best Friends and Bullies

Mrs. Long came out on the porch, "I guess you heard our news. We are so grateful to the Lord for providing in this area. It's not very far from here – over on Maple Street. The church is a rather sizable brick building. The parsonage is a large white house with a wide front porch. It's an old house, but it is in remarkable condition."

"I think I know that house. Is it the one that has had the 'For Sale' sign out for several months?"

"I believe it is," said Mrs. Long

"At my parents' fiftieth wedding anniversary several months ago, we were talking about it. I believe my parents were married in that house. Mother came down an immense staircase located on the left side of the living room. It's apparently visible from the front door."

"I went with my husband to see the house, and I believe I remember seeing such a staircase."

"That must be the house then. It's the only church with a house for sale in that area."

Corrie couldn't believe her ears. She looked at Lizzie; each of them seemed to know what the other was thinking. That house would be unique in many ways.

They knew they would have grand times playing in and exploring the house that was well over fifty years old.

Chapter 7

Summer's Fun

As Corrie and her parents sat around the table enjoying a leisurely supper, Corrie inquired about their upcoming vacation.

"Mom, do I have this right? We're going to Canada to see Auntie Maude and Uncle Harry, and then we're going up to see the World's Fair? Where is it again?"

"It's in Montreal, Quebec and it's called Expo 67."

"Will we get to see Tippy, too?"

"I imagine so."

"I hope so. I really like her. Remember we took Little Bit over to their house and Tippy chased her around the table. That was so funny. When are we leaving?"

"It will be around the second week in July."

"Cool, I think Lizzie is leaving then, too."

"Corrie, there is something else we have to talk about. I have decided to take a full-time job in the medical department. During the summer, I will work two or three days a week, but when school starts, I will begin working full time."

Corrie's eyes clouded as she said, "Who will stay with me?"

Best Friends and Bullies

"We have several options during the summer – you will be spending some time with Lizzie and some time with your grandparents. Once school starts, we have a housekeeper and nanny coming to work for us. I will need help with the house, and we really don't want you coming home alone. Do you know Bessie who works for the Harpers?"

"I've never met her, but I've seen her standing at the door of their house when I go to school. She always smiles and waves at me."

"Their girls are in high school now, and she wants to get another job."

"And she's coming here?"

"That's the plan."

"I guess that will be okay," Corrie was still non-committal.

"We can talk later. Right now, we need to finish supper so we can get to church this evening."

Corrie usually enjoyed the children's program, but it was becoming increasingly hard to put up with the boys that attended and sat in the back of the room. They were always saying rude and unkind things to her, especially since she got the brace. Because her walking was a bit unsteady, they liked to call out to her, "Waddle, waddle, quack, quack." Corrie did her best to ignore them, but it really bothered her. Her favorite thing about church was the teacher, Mr. Sam. He really knew how to teach and talk to kids her age. It was too bad that he never heard the boys speaking unkindly and Corrie was far too embarrassed to tell him, lest he thinks she was a big baby.

As she walked out of the room, she heard one of the boys, call out "Waddle, waddle, quack, quack. You are fatter and clumsier than ever, Clumsy Corrie."

Summer's Fun

Mr. Sam heard this time and moved to silence the offenders. Corrie quickly made her escape before the tears could start falling. In fact, she was able to wait until she and her parents arrived home before bursting into tears. They inquired about the torrent of emotions, and through her tears, Corrie began to explain.

"The boys, Joey, Barry, Andy, and Matt that sit in the back, they usually say mean things to me about how I walk, how fat I am, and stuff like that. Tonight, they were saying, "Waddle, waddle, quack, quack!" They actually made duck noises at me. I was so embarrassed. I think Mr. Sam was yelling at them for it, but I was so embarrassed that I just left in a hurry."

Mr. and Mrs. Cushman looked at each other. They had been expecting something like this at some point. They were unhappy that it had occurred at church, a place where they wanted her to relax, be happy, and to feel safe. Mr. Cushman looked at his daughter, and said, "Corrie, we are very sorry that this happened, but you have to realize that people are going to be mean. It's too bad that it happens at church. I don't suppose we should call their parents?"

"Daddy, don't do that. They would think I was an awful tattletale and a cry baby, too. I can't believe I cried tonight. I'm so embarrassed."

"I won't call this time, but if they keep it up, I will have no choice. I don't want you this upset every time we go to church. I know Mr. Sam is handling the misbehavior, but sooner or later you are going to have to tell him what's going on with you. You have nothing to be ashamed of."

Corrie sniffled and managed to give her father a hug and say, "Thanks, Daddy. I'll remember."

Best Friends and Bullies

He released her from the hug and said, "Now how about a snack? I think I know where some of your favorite cookies are. "

Corrie gave a half-grin and said, "That sounds good. Want me to pour us some milk?"

Her mother joined them, and the three of them snacked and talked. She remarked, "Did you know we had a pet duck when I was a little girl?"

"No. I knew Grandpa had chickens because you told me you used to help him clean out the chicken coops. Yuck! But a pet duck? That is so cool! What was its name?"

"His name was Herman."

"Where did Herman live? Did Grandpa build him a duck pond?"

"No, he didn't have a duck pond, but do you want to know something hilarious? Our next-door neighbor, Mrs. Cahill, had a fishpond. Our chickens really enjoyed splashing in the water and would wander over there. When they did, Herman would start squawking and quacking. Of course, someone in the house had to go and retrieve them. Herman was better than any watchdog."

"What happened to Herman?"

"He died of old age."

It had never occurred to Corrie that her parents had pets when they were children, but the story of Herman piqued her curiosity. "Did you have any pets, Daddy?"

"I always had a dog. I remember one, in particular, whose name was Jack. He used to pull me around the yard in a little cart. I also used to share my ice cream cone with him. I'd take a lick. He'd take a lick."

Summer's Fun

Corrie wrinkled her nose and said, "Ewww, dog germs. I like dogs, but not that much. Well, thanks for the stories. I guess I better go to bed. Mom, you will be here when I get up in the morning, won't you?"

"I will, but we need to talk about Friday. Do you need help with Goofball?"

"Yes, please."

Corrie and her mother left the room to prepare for bed. Once she was in bed, she grabbed her book and started reading. She had thirty minutes to read before she had to turn out her light.

The next morning Corrie was awakened by the sound of her parents talking in the kitchen. She wasn't that interested in their conversation, but as she neared the kitchen, she heard her mother say, "I'm sure my working is the right thing to do, but Corrie seems so worried about it. I think it goes deeper than just my going to work. I wish she would tell us what's really going on."

Corrie paused before she went into the kitchen because she did not want her parents to know she had heard their conversation. She wasn't sure what was going on herself and why she was so afraid all of the time. Corrie walked into the kitchen just in time to give her dad a goodbye kiss as he walked out the door. As she sat down at the kitchen table to talk with her mother, her mother asked, "Did you have a good sleep?"

"I did, but Mom, I had some weird dreams. Something was chasing me, but I don't know what. I was happy to wake up this morning."

"Did you read a happy book, a scary book, or a sad book before you went to bed?"

Best Friends and Bullies

"I was reading Nancy Drew. They are always a little scary, but she always wins in the end."

"Maybe you need to read something a little happier at night. We'll work on finding you some happier books. Would you like to go to the library this morning?"

"I would LOVE to go to the library today!"

"Okay, we will. Now, how about some breakfast?"

"Can I have a piece of cheese toast?"

"I think that sounds good. I think I will join you."

After breakfast, Corrie straightened her room and dressed for the day. As usual, her mother helped her with Goofball. Once she was dressed, the two of them went to the kitchen to discuss supper. The plan was to make a meatloaf and baked potatoes since that was Mr. Cushman's favorite. They needed to pick up some fresh vegetables at the produce stand while they were out.

"Mom, may I make a dessert or at least help?"

"What did you have in mind?"

"Could we make a strawberry cobbler? That's easy, and Daddy likes that."

"Let's see if we can find strawberries when we go to the produce stand."

Corrie went back to her room and lost herself in the world of Nancy Drew. Somehow it wasn't as scary in the daylight. She was totally engrossed in trying to solve the mystery before Nancy did, but she was more troubled by the absence of Nancy's mother than by the dangers she encountered. Corrie thought she remembered reading that Nancy's mother had died in a car accident when Nancy was really young. That really bothered her and made it difficult

Summer's Fun

for her to enjoy the books entirely. She had just figured out the mystery and finished the book when her mother called her to go on their errands.

Their first stop was the produce stand where Corrie was thrilled to find the fresh strawberries that she needed. Mrs. Cushman was equally happy to see some green beans. It would be a busy afternoon, but Corrie knew she would have fun with her mother in the kitchen.

The next stop was the public library. Corrie climbed out of the car and began to walk toward the library hurriedly. Mrs. Cushman called out, "Corrie, wait! Let's go in together."

Corrie stopped and waited for her mother. Then the two of them walked into the children's room of the library together.

"Do you need my help choosing some books?"

"That's okay, I think I'll just browse a little, but I will check with you on the books I want to take."

Corrie wandered among the shelves looking at this book and then that book. She was drawn to one she found toward the back of the fiction section. It looked like it was about two best friends. She briefly looked through the first chapter and discovered that the main character had both parents still living – perhaps this would be a safe book and she could probably share it with Lizzie. While she was there, she pulled a couple of others in the series off the shelf. She figured these would keep her busy at least for the next week or at least for the next couple of days. She took the three selected books to her mother for approval and then went to see if there were any mystery books she had not read. She chose a couple of those and decided to ask Lizzie for advice on safe books she had read and enjoyed. Surely

Best Friends and Bullies

Lizzie would understand; she just hoped that her parents never found out how afraid she was of losing them.

When the books were checked out, Corrie and her mother returned home. It was time for a sandwich, and Corrie was confident that her mother made the best toasted bologna and cheese sandwiches ever. Corrie got the pickles and Kool-Aid out of the refrigerator as her mother made the sandwiches. She also pulled some chips out of the pantry. It was one of her favorite lunches. Before they ate, her mother offered a blessing.

As they were enjoying their lunch, Mrs. Cushman said, "Do you remember that I am working tomorrow and the next day and that you are staying with Lizzie?"

"Oh, yeah. I had forgotten that. I can't wait to see the Long's new house. I can't believe she is living where Grandma got married. That is so cool!"

"Daddy and I will ride together since we are both working at the same place. We will drop you off at Lizzie's about 7:30. Mrs. Long said you could have breakfast with them. You will need to get up around 7:00 so I can help you with Goofball and getting dressed. You will need to get everything together that you are taking and put it in the front hall tonight."

Corrie and her mother began supper preparations. Mrs. Cushman capped and sliced the strawberries. She instructed Corrie about how much sugar and butter to put in, and then she put them in a pie plate. Once that was complete, they covered it with a crust and put it in the oven. While the cobbler was cooking, the two of them strung and snapped the green beans. Once the beans were ready to cook, Corrie asked her mother if she could visit Maggie, who lived across the street. Having been granted permission to do so, she walked across the street and rang the doorbell of her friend's house.

Maggie's mother answered the door, with the words. "Hello, Corrie, we haven't seen you lately."

"I know. I've been kind of busy. I've had doctors appointments for my brace and Mom is working more, and I can't stay at home alone. So, I've been staying with friends. Is Maggie here?"

"I think she's down in the basement playroom. Why don't you go on down?"

Corrie walked carefully down the stairs clinging to the handrail, but before she made it to the bottom or could say anything, Maggie called to her, "Hey, Corrie come on down. I have something to show you."

As Corrie stepped into the basement, Maggie ran over to Corrie with an 8-Ball in her hand and said, "Look at this. It is so cool. It can tell you what is going to happen."

"Aww, nobody but God knows what is going to happen."

"This ball does. Ask it a question, but it can only be answered with a yes or no."

"This is crazy, but I'll try. Here goes. Is my name, Corrie?"

Maggie shook the ball and turned it over. When she saw the answer, she handed it to Corrie, "See, here it says, 'yes.' Ask another one, and you hold it this time."

Corrie took the ball and asked, "Do I have a dog?" Then she took it, shook it and turned it over just as Maggie had.

When she turned it over, she saw the answer, "Not at this time."

"Wow, that's really something."

When Maggie saw her interest, she said, "This is a special one. It's the deluxe model. It can talk. We just have to be in the right room. Lets' go upstairs to my sister's room. The reception is best there."

Corrie wasn't sure that she should go along with Maggie's plan, but she still followed Maggie to her sister's room. Maggie moved much more quickly than Corrie, so she was in the bedroom a minute or so before she was. She noticed that Maggie's mother was there, but assumed she was there to be sure the girls didn't harm any of Maggie's sister's belongings. Maggie handed her the ball, saying, "Go ahead, ask it questions about your vacation. You are going on vacation, aren't you?"

"Yes, but what else do I need to know?"

"Just ask it some questions. Remember, yes or no questions."

"Okay, here goes. Are we going on vacation?"

"Yes," the ball replied.

"Will we have fun?"

"Yes."

"Will I get to see Tippy?"

"Yes."

"Will anything bad happen?"

"Yes."

"Will I get hurt?"

"Yes."

"Will my parents get hurt?"

Summer's Fun

"Yes."

"Will I die?"

"No."

"Will my mom die?"

"Yes."

"Will my daddy die?"

"Yes."

"Will it happen in Canada?"

"Yes."

"Will I be with Auntie Maude and Uncle Harry?"

"No."

"Will I be at the fair?"

"Yes."

"What will happen to me," Corrie was near tears and so upset that she forgot about the yes or no questions.

The ball didn't answer. Corrie threw the ball on the bed and ran out of the room and then the house. Maggie and her mother looked at each other in horror as Maggie's older sister came out from under the bed. They had never expected their little prank to have this effect.

When Corrie got home, her mother noticed that she looked a little strained, so she suggested that Corrie take a rest and read her one of her books. Corrie grabbed one of her library books and went out to the swing in the back yard. She was soon engrossed in the story of two girls who became best friends when one of them moved to a new school. It reminded her of what had happened to her and Lizzie. Soon she was daydreaming about the fun she and Lizzie had had that summer – the worm hunt and the walk to the drug store. She just wished they could have taken a dip in the creek before Lizzie moved, but Lizzie's new house sounded so cool.

Her thoughts were interrupted when she heard her mother call, "Corrie, it's time to set the table." She was really excited about the cobbler she had helped make. She just hoped that her daddy would like it. As she set the table, she was careful to put every utensil in its place. She wanted the table to look really lovely, not that it was a special occasion other than the fact that this was the first time she had really helped prepare supper. The meal was ready shortly after Mr. Cushman came in from work. He bragged about the meal and especially the strawberry cobbler, saying it was the best he had ever eaten. Corrie beamed; it felt so good to have her parents happy with her.

Chapter 8

Lizzie's New House

The next morning Corrie's mother woke her up. At first, Corrie wondered why she was being called so early, but then she realized that she was spending the day with Lizzie. Her mother helped her put Goofball on, and then she dressed for the day. Corrie walked into the kitchen, ate the graham cracker and drank the juice her mother put out for her, and then returned to her bedroom to finish getting ready, A few minutes later her mother called, "It's time to go!" Corrie came out of her room, picked up her backpack in the front hall, and followed her mother out to the car.

Corrie chattered all the way to Lizzie's house about how excited she was to spend the day with her friend, but as she talked her face clouded over, and she began to ask questions, "How far do you have to walk into the building? How far do you have to drive from Lizzie's house?"

Her mother interrupted the barrage of questions by saying, "I'll be fine. Just have fun with Lizzie and obey Mrs. Long."

"Okay, Mom. I will."

They completed the rest of the ride in silence. When they arrived at the Long's house, Corrie grabbed her backpack and kissed her mother goodbye, and climbed out of the car. Her mother followed her as they walked to the house and knocked on the door. Mrs. Long opened the door and welcomed them in.

Mrs. Cushman began, "I sorry we are barging in on you so early in the morning."

Mrs. Long interrupted her, "No need to apologize. Dan and I are early risers. We enjoy lingering over coffee and our Bible reading." She looked at Corrie and continued, "Now Lizzie is another story. She is a real sleepyhead during the summer months. She'll be up soon."

Corrie interjected, "Oh, that's all right, I have a book to read. That will be fun."

With those words, Mrs. Cushman realized she had to leave to get to work on time. With a final hug and kiss for her daughter, she got in her car and left.

Mrs. Long turned to Corrie and said, "Can I get you some breakfast?"

"No thank you, but can I sit in one of the chairs out in the yard and read until Lizzie gets up?"

"Sure thing. Just make yourself at home."

Corrie grabbed one of her books and settled down in the chosen chair. Soon she was lost in the adventures of the main character and her best friend. She was so entranced with the action of the two girls that she was entirely unaware of the time and her surroundings. Suddenly someone grabbed her and shouted, "Boo!" and began to laugh hysterically.

Corrie was so startled that she upset the chair and landed in the grass. Lizzie immediately stopped laughing and helped her up. Corrie was a little unsteady; so, Lizzie helped her into the house. As they walked into the house,

Lizzie's New House

Lizzie asked Corrie, "Do you want anything to eat? I'm getting ready to eat breakfast. I'm going to eat Cheerios and banana. Come on have some with me."

"Maybe I'll have a little. Mom made me eat some breakfast before we left the house."

"What did you have?"

"I had a graham cracker and some juice."

"That's not enough. Don't you know that every day must start with a delicious and balanced breakfast?"

"Maybe, but I don't like breakfast."

The girls sat down to bowls of Cheerios. After the blessing, they began to eat in silence. Corrie could tell Lizzie was trying really hard not to be silly and she appreciated that – it lessened the likelihood of her choking.

Corrie finally broke the silence by asking, "What are we doing first? I sure want to see your room."

Lizzie grinned as she replied, "I want you to see it. We can go right up after breakfast because I have to make my bed. I was in a hurry to get down and see you; so, I haven't made it yet."

"You know bed-making is overrated. Why make it when you're just going to get back in it at night? Too bad my parents don't see it that way."

The two girls finished breakfast and rinsed their dishes, put them in the drainer and began making their way upstairs.

"Oh, Lizzie, I love these stairs. I can just see my Grandma descending them in her wedding dress. I wonder if Grandpa watched her as she came down. I bet he looked like Prince Charming waiting for Cinderella."

Best Friends and Bullies

They walked into Lizzie's room together, and they made her bed. Then, Corrie walked over and looked out the window and remarked, "Wow! You can see the church from your room, and it has a steeple! Steeples are so cool!"

"We have a bell, too. We can walk over and see the church if you want to."

"I think that would be really neat."

"Is there anything up here you want to see?"

"No, but I would like to get a good look at the stairs again. I was so busy thinking about Grandma and Grandpa when we came up."

"Okay, Corrie what are you thinking?"

"I just thought that if we could find some cushions, we could sit on them and slide down the steps."

"Why would we do that?"

"We can pretend we are sledding down a hill. Doesn't that sound like fun?"

"Corrie, you're crazy, but we'll try it, but then I have a GREAT idea!"

The two girls made their way down the stairs and walked over to the deacon's bench, removed the long cushion, and walked to the top of the stairs carrying it between them. Lizzie carefully laid it on the floor at the top of the stairs. Corrie sat on the front of the cushion and Lizzie on the back. Lizzie pushed off by clutching the railing and pushing off. With that, they slid down the stairs. The resounding crash of their landing brought Mrs. Long running.

"Girls, girls, what happened?"

Corrie looked up at her and said, "Oh, don't worry Mrs. Long, we were just pretending we were sledding."

Lizzie's New House

Lizzie added, "We didn't hurt anything, Mom. See the cushion is intact."

"Yes, but are you all right? That was highly dangerous. Put the cushion back on the deacon's bench and sit down until lunchtime."

Both girls replied, "Yes, ma'am," and obediently sat down on the bench.

Corrie looked over at Lizzie and remarked, "Well, that idea flopped. What was yours?"

"The church and this house have to be over 50 years old. I just bet there is a secret passage between the two."

"Lizzie, whatever made you think of that?"

"Well, Nancy Drew is always finding secret passages in houses. I just figured there just might be one here. Think of the fun we could have if there really is one."

"Lizzie, I really think we need to ask permission before we go poking around. Your mother wasn't thrilled when we slid down the stairs. I don't want to do anything to upset her."

'Corrie, I keep telling you that you worry too much, but if it makes you happy, I'll bring it up at lunch today. It'll be fine, you'll see."

At that minute, Mrs. Long called the girls to lunch. They came to the table eager to eat, but also to divulge their latest idea. Before they ate, they recited a traditional blessing together, and then Mr. Long added a few words of his own. Corrie listened with a certain longing; she really wished she knew God like that. Her thought was interrupted by Mrs. Long, handing her a bowl of chili. She was offered slaw and cornbread as well, and as she ate hungrily, she heard Lizzie ask, "Mom, Daddy, Corrie and I were wondering something."

"What's that, Liz?"

"Well, you know this house is super old. I really think that there just might be a secret passageway over to the church. We want to explore the closets and see what we can find."

"And if you find one, what will you do?"

"Follow it!"

"Here's the deal. You and Corrie may check the closets in your room and the spare room. If you find any stairs, you must ask your mother or me before you follow them."

"Okay, Daddy, we will."

After eating lunch and helping with the dishes, the two girls went upstairs to begin their search in the closets for a secret passageway. First, they went to Lizzie's room and opened her closet door. Lizzie pushed her clothes aside, and the two girls began to crawl around on the floor looking for loose boards or a trap door.

"Lizzie, I have an idea. Why don't we look for a secret panel in the wall? There might be one of those as well."

"That's a great idea, but let's try looking for a secret passage first."

The girls resumed their search and were excited to discover a few loose boards, but neither girl had the strength to pull them up. Lizzie looked at Corrie and said, "Oh, that's okay, I'll ask Daddy to help me tonight. Let's look for a secret panel, and then we will go to the spare room and check that closet."

Much to their disappointment, the girls could not find anything resembling a secret panel in Lizzie's closet, so they moved on to the next closet. There were definitely no loose floorboards, but they held out hope when they found a loose board in the wall, but Lizzie thought she had better ask before they attempted to remove it.

They walked back into Lizzie's room and collapsed on the floor beside her bed. Corrie turned to Lizzie and asked, "Do you ever worry that something will happen to your parents?"

"No, not really. There are times I might think about it, like when they drive my sister to college or like when they took her to that Christian camp to work this summer. We were still in school, and they drove to the camp and back in one day while I was in school."

"I am so afraid that something will happen to my parents, especially Mom, and I will never see her again."

"Have you told your parents?"

"No, I am embarrassed to talk to them, but actually it gets worse. I really don't know if I'm saved. I just don't remember anything about asking Jesus to save me. I'm so scared and so embarrassed. I do remember being baptized, but I also remember I didn't know what to say. What should I do?"

"Corrie, you have to talk to your parents. Tell them what you're thinking and feeling. It's no good to keep crying whenever your parents leave. You've got to talk to them."

"I know, but what will they say?"

"They'll be glad you told them what's bothering you."

"If only I knew they would not be mad or disappointed."

"Corrie, they love you. Promise me you'll tell them."

"Okay, I'll tell them tonight."

Best Friends and Bullies

With that, the girls turned to the books they had been reading. Soon it was time for Corrie's mother to come. As she walked out the door, Lizzie mouthed the words, "Tell them."

Corrie nodded and followed her mom out the door.

As they left, Corrie turned to Lizzie and called, "See you tomorrow."

Chapter 9

Corrie's Confession

Corrie walked out to the car with her mother and climbed in beside her. "How was your day?" her mother asked.

"It was fun. We looked for secret passages and secret panels in Lizzie's closet. Lizzie's house is really old. It would be so much fun to find something."

"I see you are putting your Nancy Drew skills to work. Just don't start scaring yourselves."

"We won't, but a secret panel or secret passage would be so cool. Grandma's house has sort of a secret passage in her bedroom and the front room. You know when you go in her closet and go through to the front bedroom."

"Have fun, but remember to ask a grown-up before you follow any passages," her mother warned.

"We will. Mr. Long already made us promise."

"Good. Now, what shall we have for supper? How does brupper sound? We have eggs, and some bacon needs to be eaten. I can cook up some grits or hash browns and open a can of biscuits."

Corrie said, "That sounds really good. Let's let Daddy choose between grits and hash browns. Mom, there's something I need to talk about with you and Daddy after supper."

Best Friends and Bullies

They arrived home and pulled into the carport, got out of the car, and walked into the house together. Mrs. Cushman went to change out of her nurse's uniform while Corrie washed her hands and began to pull the ingredients out of the refrigerator. Supper was well underway by the time Mr. Cushman got home. He chose hash browns which was okay with Corrie. That meant she got to have more ketchup.

After supper, the family worked together to clean the kitchen. There were no leftovers, so clean-up consisted of putting the dirty dishes in the dishwasher. As they put the last plate in and turned it on, Mrs. Cushman turned to her husband and said, "Corrie said she has something to talk to us about."

Mr. Cushman turned to his daughter and said affectionately, "Well, what do you say we go into the living room and sit down together, and you can tell us what's on your mind?"

The family went together into the living room. Her parents sat on the loveseat, and Corrie sat at their feet. Corrie looked up at her parents and began to cry. When she could muster the words, she said to her parents, "I'm not sure how to tell you, but I'm just not sure I'm saved. I know I was baptized when Pastor Anderson was here, but I just don't remember anything."

Her dad looked at her and said, "Corrie, let me ask you a question. What if God should say to you, 'Why should I let you into Heaven?'"

"I guess I would say, I try to follow the rules, and I've been baptized."

"Corrie, that won't work. Let's see what God tells us in the Bible. Can you go to your room and get your Bible and

Corrie's Confession

the little *Wordless Book* that Auntie Maude gave you before they moved to Canada?"

Corrie got up and went to her room to retrieve the requested items. She resumed her place at her parents' feet. She handed her dad the books. Her dad gave the Bible back to her. He opened the little *Wordless Book* to the gold page and began. "This page reminds us of God. Corrie, can you turn to Genesis 1:1 and tell me what it says."

Corrie turned to the passage and said, "It says, God created everything in the beginning."

"What does that mean?"

"God made everything."

"Yes, but anything else? Don't you see that no one made God? He's always been around."

"Yes, I know that nobody made God."

"Now look at Revelation 4:7. What does that say?"

"It looks like a prayer telling God He is worthy to receive our praise. Is that because He is in charge of everything?"

"Right. God is in charge of everything because He is in control of everything. He is the King of the world and expects obedience. Now turn to the black page. Also look up Romans 3:23."

Corrie turned to both as her dad asked her, "What does it say?"

"It says that everyone has sinned and fallen short of God's glory. I know sin is the bad stuff I do, but what does it mean to fall short of God's glory?"

"It means no matter how good you try to be; you can never be as good as God wants you to be – as good as you have to be to get to Heaven or to have a relationship with Him. Think of it like this, if you took a rock and threw it to the school, could you make it?"

"No, I don't think so."

"That's how it is when you try to meet God's standard of doing right. You just can't do it."

"But, Daddy, I've tried so hard to be good. Won't that work?"

"Is it good enough if you have been assigned to throw the stone to the school at the end of the street, but it only makes it to Maggie's front yard?"

"No, I guess not."

"It's the same way with what God expects of you. He wants you to be as good as Jesus, but you just can't do it."

"So then, what happens?"

"Can you turn to Romans 5:8 and the red page?

Corrie did as her dad asked her and read what it said.

She read that God had shown His love for us by sending His Son to die for us. Then she looked at her dad and noted, "I guess that's what the red page means. That Jesus died, but why did He have to?"

Her dad replied, "Corrie, listen to me. This is very important. You can't reach God's expectations because you've broken His rules, and you have to be punished. Jesus took that punishment by dying on the cross for you, but when He died and came back from the dead, He made something possible. Turn to the white page and turn to 2 Corinthians 5:21."

As Corrie turned to the passage in her Bible, he asked, "Can you tell me what that says?"

Corrie's Confession

"It says Jesus became sin for us even though He was perfect, but it also said He gave us His righteousness. That means God calls us righteous, rather than naming our sins."

"Have you sinned?"

Tears welled up in Corrie's eyes. "Yes, Daddy, I have. I got mad at God because of the NF and Goofball, but I think I sinned more by trying to be good enough all by myself."

"You're right. You have sinned. But now you've read that Jesus died to take care of your sin. Now you need to do something. Turn to Romans 10:13, what does it say?"

"It says if I call on Him, Jesus will save me and give me His righteousness. I don't think I've ever done that."

"That's right, now what do you want to do?"

"Can I ask Him right now?"

"Certainly." Together they knelt as Corrie asked the Lord for His gift of salvation, and each of her parents prayed that God would bless her and that she would continue to follow His leading. The three of them stood and hugged, Corrie felt as though a huge weight had been lifted from her heart. She had not felt so happy in a long time.

That night Corrie went to bed with a happy heart and woke up happy the next morning. She was so pleased, she forgot to worry about her mother's job because she was so excited to share her decision with Lizzie. When her mother called her, she got right up. Even Goofball did not seem so bad. She had her regular graham cracker and juice for early breakfast since she would be eating again with Lizzie.

When she arrived at the Long's house, she climbed out of the car and walked to the house and tapped lightly on the kitchen door. The Longs were in the kitchen drinking coffee and having their morning prayers. Corrie asked if she could wait in the chairs under the tree with her book until Lizzie awakened. The Longs gave their permission, so she found her favorite spot under the trees and began to read. She was deeply involved in the actions of the main character and her attempts to win a cooking contest when Lizzie snuck up on her, and in a deep voice unlike her own said, "Good morning! How about joining me for breakfast?"

Corrie jumped and let out a little scream. Lizzie burst into laughter and helped her out of the chair where she was sitting. "Come on. Somebody gave us a box of frozen waffles and some homemade jam. Breakfast is going to be so good this morning."

The two girls sat down to their waffles and jam. As they had anticipated, it was delicious. As they were savoring breakfast, Corrie looked at Lizzie and said, "I have something special to tell you."

When breakfast was over, the two girls rinsed their plates and put them in the dishwasher. Then they went out and sat under the trees. Lizzie looked at Corrie and said, "Okay, so what's the big secret?"

Corrie looked at Lizzie and said, "I asked Jesus to be my Savior last night. I was trying to get to Heaven my own way by trying to be good. I know I can't do it that way. I believed He died to take my sin away, and He did. I'm saved!"

"Oh, Corrie that is so special. Am I the first person you have told?"

"Yes. Hey, Lizzie when were you saved?"

"Let's see. It was my third birthday. My two older sisters had really spoiled me, and I really liked getting my own way. When I wanted more cake and didn't get it, I had a temper tantrum. I guess it was loud. So, Daddy took me to my bedroom and put me down for a nap. A little later Mom came in to talk to me. She asked me what happened. I told her I had been bad. I told her I felt terrible about it because I really loved Daddy. Then she told me that my badness was sin and Jesus died because of it. That's when I asked Jesus to save me, so we celebrate them both every year. You know you should really write last night's date in your Bible with the words, 'I was saved on this day.'"

"Lizzie, that's a great idea. I will do it as soon as I get home. I wish I had put my Bible in my backpack. That way, I could write it in my Bible now. Guess what? Next week we are having VBS at church. Mr. Sam, who is the best teacher ever, is teaching the class. He did say he's bringing a special guest on one of the days. I do have to warn you about the boys in the class. Most of them are disgusting."

"Boys, in general, are disgusting. My big sister says I will change my mind one of these days, but I don't think so. She's in love, and it is so mushy that it's gross."

"Yeah, I hope I never fall in love. I've watched older people kiss, and it sure is yucky."

"Oh, guess what, Corrie? Last night Daddy moved that loose board, and there really are steps in my closet. He went down them and looked around. There really is a secret passage in my closet. He said he would go with us after lunch and walk down there."

"That sounds good, but are you sure I won't fall down there?"

"That's why Daddy is going with us. He'll make sure you don't fall. Why are you so afraid of falling?"

"When I was little, I was shopping with my mom. One minute I was standing beside her in a store, and the next,

Best Friends and Bullies

I was falling down some steps into a dark basement. Somebody must have left the door open, and I lost my balance. I didn't get hurt bad, but my head really hurt."

"That sounds awful. No wonder you're so afraid of falling."

"Do you think it will be okay with my parents?

"Corrie! Would you stop worrying? You're at my house, and my parents are in charge. It'll be fine."

"Okay, but what do you want to do until then?"

"I know, Daddy visits shut-ins tomorrow. Those are old people who can't leave their houses, because they are too old or too sick. I think it would be cool to make cards to take to them. Mom has a craft box, and we can use some of that stuff to make them."

"Okay, but I'm not very good."

"Would you stop saying stuff like that?"

"Okay, what do you want me to do?"

"Go to my bedroom and get the construction paper and markers I put on my bed. Grab my Bible, so we can look up verses to write in the cards. We can work on the table in the bonus room."

Corrie went up to Lizzie's room and got the markers and paper. By the time she got to the bonus room, Lizzie was making piles of the necessary crafting items. She put the paper and the Bible on the table, and the girls got to work on their cards. By the time Mrs. Long called them to lunch, the girls had made five cards each and were rather pleased with their work.

After lunch and clean up, the girls were ready to explore the secret passage. They went upstairs to wait for Mr. Long. Lizzie opened her closet and pushed the clothes aside. As she did so, she said, "I forgot to tell you, we found a secret panel, too. We opened it, but I wanted you to be here to see if there was anything in it. Let's look while we wait for Daddy."

"It's your closet, you go first."

Lizzie opened the panel and reached in. Her hands touched something, and she pulled it out. It looked like a diary, and it looked like it was written by a girl their age. The front page said, "The Diary of Anna Katherine Parker. When this you see, remember me. My Diary for 1942."

Corrie looked at it and said, "Wow! This is old. It was written when my mom was a little girl."

Lizzie looked at it and said, "This will be such fun to read together. Let me see if there is anything else in there." She put her hand back in the hole and said. "No, I don't feel anything else."

By that time, Mr. Long had joined them. The girls proudly showed him the diary, and he shared their enthusiasm. He turned to them and said, "I guess this means we don't need to look in the secret passage."

Lizzie replied emphatically, "Daddy! Of course, we do. Now more than ever."

Mr. Long said, "All right. Here is how we are going to do it. I will go first with my flashlight. Then I will shine it on the steps so that each of you can see where you are going. Lizzie, I want you to follow me. Corrie, when she is halfway down, you follow. Do you understand?"

Both girls looked at him and said, "Yes, sir."

They all began their descent to the basement. Corrie was surprised at how easy it was to manage the stairs with the handrail. Lizzie and her dad went ahead of her to help as it was needed. When they all arrived at the

Best Friends and Bullies

bottom of the stairs, Mr. Long showed them the room, the girls realized it was a secret room rather than a passageway leading to anywhere.

Mr. Long looked at them and said, "Girls, now you have seen this, but once we go upstairs, this room is off limits unless an adult is with you."

Both Corrie and Lizzie agreed and in unison said, "Okay." Corrie was secretly relieved. She found the room a bit creepy but did not want to admit it. They returned to Lizzie's bedroom, and both girls thanked him profusely for taking them down to see the room even if there wasn't a secret passage. They closed the door and returned the closet to its regular order. Then they picked up their books and went out under the trees to read. They had planned to save the diary for another day.

Chapter 10

Ebenezer

The week for Vacation Bible School finally arrived. Lizzie and Corrie could hardly wait. Corrie had given such glowing reports of past years that Lizzie was beyond excited about Mr. Sam, about the crafts, and about the whole experience in general. The first day was like organized pandemonium – there were more children there than anyone had anticipated. They had to create more classes very quickly, but it was also apparent there were not enough craft supplies. Corrie was more than happy to give up her space at the craft table because she felt like her craft attempts always looked like junkyard specials. She was, however, glad to pass out the glue, markers, construction paper, pipe cleaners, and beads. The only table she dreaded was the one with those obnoxious boys who continually tormented and teased her.

As she approached the table where Joey, Barry, and Dan were sitting, Joey mouthed the words, "Quack, quack" at her.

Barry put out his foot in an attempt to trip her, but she managed to see it and avoid falling by grabbing the table as she avoided his foot. The boys looked at each other and grinned mischievously. Corrie moved away from them as quickly as possible. Mr. Sam noticed the actions and proceeded to rebuke the boys.

Best Friends and Bullies

Corrie was so glad when craft time was over, and it was time for Bible class. This year they were studying the first 11 chapters of Genesis. Mr. Sam said knowing that portion of Scripture is foundational to understanding the Bible.

A lady who was using a walker was standing next to Mr. Sam. He gestured to her and said, "Class, I want you to meet my cousin, Sadie. She has a friend with her; his name is Ebenezer. If you want to know why she has him, you can ask her during snack time, but first I want to give you a challenge to find out about his name. It's in the Bible. She's going to be helping me teach the lessons this week. Every day, we will answer two questions as we study the lessons. What does this teach me about God, and how should I respond to this knowledge?"

As they dove into the first chapter of Genesis, they discovered how God made the entire world out of nothing – how He created everything in six literal days – and how He put Adam and Eve, the first man and woman in a beautiful garden. They all concluded that they learned that God could do anything and that their response should be to trust Him about everything in their lives.

They all filed out for snack time after the Bible lesson. Corrie grabbed Lizzie and said, "Let's walk out with Miss Sadie. I want to know about Ebenezer."

The two girls walked up to her and said, "Miss Sadie, will you walk with us to snack time, please. We want to hear about Ebenezer."

"What do you want to know?"

Corrie began, "Why do you have him?"

"Because I have balance issues that relate to headaches and back problems, so I need help walking."

Ebenezer

Corrie nodded, but continued, "I know this is personal and I could get in trouble for asking it, but I see a lot of bumps on your hands. Do you have NF?"

Miss Sadie looked at her in surprise and said, "I do, but what do you know about NF?"

Corrie said, "I have it too. I have to wear this dumb brace, but I named him Goofball because he is goofing up my life. Why did you name your walker a cool name like Ebenezer? When I was in third grade, we read a story about a farmer who had a tractor named Ebenezer. I really liked that name."

Miss Sadie hid a smile as she said, "Oh, I see. I'll tell you what. Look for Ebenezer's name in the Bible. I would suggest using a concordance. That's a book that lists keywords in the Bible and lists Bible verses where they are found. When you find it, we will talk again."

By that time, they had arrived at the snack table. Various ladies from the church had made homemade cookies; today, they had chocolate chip cookies. Lizzie, Corrie and Miss Sadie all dug in. After all, who could resist a chocolate chip cookie?

As they walked into the closing session after a time of games, which Corrie hated, she turned to Lizzie and said, "Do your parents have one of those concordances that Miss Sadie was talking about?"

"I think so. We can ask when my parents pick us up."

When the Longs arrived at the church to pick up the girls, they were full of talk about everything they had done that day. Corrie nudged Lizzie and sent a message with her eyes, which prompted her to ask, "Daddy, do you know what a concordance is?"

"Yes, Lizzie, I do. Do you?"

Best Friends and Bullies

"It's a book you can use to look up words in the Bible and find Bible verses that use them."

"Why do you ask?"

Corrie answered, "She's really asking for me, Mr. Long. Mr. Sam's cousin, Miss Sadie, is visiting him, and she came to VBS this morning. Miss Sadie walks with a walker that she named Ebenezer. She said the name is from the Bible and that we could find it by using a concordance. We were hoping you had one we could use."

"As a matter of fact, I have several. We can look at them together after lunch."

They continued to talk about VBS during lunch. Then Mr. Long and the girls went over to the church to his study. He pulled a book off the shelf; it was one of the biggest books that either girl had ever seen. Mr. Long laid it on his desk and began to flip the pages. As he did so, he began to explain, "A concordance is arranged very much like a dictionary, but it is very different. Some of the entries explain the meanings of the words. This is one of those. Now turn to the "E" section. Once you get there, look for the word Ebenezer."

They found the word Ebenezer quickly. As they poured over the list, Corrie looked up and asked, "What are those funny-looking letters by the word?"

Mr. Long replied, "That's the Hebrew translation of it. The Old Testament was written in Hebrew. We don't have to worry about that right now. We just need the reference where it is found in the Bible."

Corrie and Lizzie looked at the list of references. As they searched, they determined that the verse they were searching for was 1 Samuel 7:12. Lizzie looked up and said,

Ebenezer

"Daddy, do you have a piece of paper that we can write this reference down? Then, Corrie and I can look it up. "

Mr. Long produced a piece of paper, and Lizzie wrote down the reference. They left his office hurriedly so that they could look up the reference. As they left, they yelled, "Thank you!"

They ran back to the house, but as they got there, Lizzie turned to Corrie and said, "I'll go in and get our Bibles and then we can look up the verse."

Corrie went over to the chairs under the tree and waited for Lizzie. She was back quickly and had the Bibles with her. Corrie eagerly took hers because she was quick at Bible drills and had had lots of practice. She found the passage first, which was 1 Samuel 7:1-12, but she waited for Lizzie before she started reading. When Lizzie found it, they began to read about a major battle between the Israelites and the Philistines. God had given them victory. Samuel set up a stone and named it Ebenezer, which means "The Lord has helped us to this point."

"Wow," said Lizzie. "That's amazing. I bet she named her walker Ebenezer to remind her that God is really her help."

"That is so cool. I can hardly wait to ask Miss Sadie tomorrow."

The next morning the girls were so excited to go to VBS. They wanted to be the first to tell Miss Sadie that they knew all about Ebenezer in the Bible. As soon as they saw her outside, they ran up to her, shouting, "Miss Sadie, Miss Sadie. We found Ebenezer in the Bible!"

Miss Sadie smiled and said, "Slow down, girls. I'm right here."

Best Friends and Bullies

Corrie opened her Bible to the place she had marked as she said, "Here it is in 1 Samuel 7:1-12. Samuel wanted a reminder of God's power in the lives of the Israelites. They fought a big battle and won. So, he found a big rock and named it Ebenezer as a reminder that the Lord had helped them with their battles. Is that why your walker is named Ebenezer?"

"Exactly, I've had some hard things happen to me, and I've had some good things happen. When I started having balance problems, I was sad. So, when I had to use a walker, I wanted it to be more like a friend, and so I named it. Actually, it's a him, because he's blue. Every time I mention his name, it's a reminder that God is my true source of help."

"I like that. Maybe I should have given Goofball another name, but maybe I can turn it into a joke."

"Goofball is fine for a name, but just remember not to be mad at others or God. When you start to have unhappy feelings, find someone you can talk to who will help you see God's hand, and help in your life."

"I will, and thank you so much. You've been so much help. Can I write to you sometime?"

"Sure. I'll tell Sam to give you my address. You can write to me anytime you want."

"That is so cool! I'll be sure to ask him."

The morning passed quickly and was rather enjoyable. Even craft time felt doable for Corrie. When they went out for snack time, Corrie noticed that Miss Sadie was sitting alone. Mr. Sam was chasing some ill-behaved boys. She motioned to Lizzie to come with her, saying, "Miss Sadie is all alone, and I have some random questions I want to ask."

Ebenezer

"Corrie, don't embarrass yourself or me."

"I won't. I just want to know what's it's like to have Mr. Sam as a cousin. Maybe it will help me deal with my cousin, Arnie. I also want to ask her about worrying about my parents."

"That sounds like a really personal conversation. I'll just sit over here and watch everyone."

"Okay, I'll be right back."

Corrie walked over to Miss Sadie, who was sitting under a tree. As she approached her, she said quietly, "Miss Sadie, can I talk to you for a few minutes?"

"Sure, what's on your mind?"

"This is kind of personal, but do you ever worry about your parents?"

"Corrie, when I was your age, I worried all the time. I was so afraid they were going to die, and I would be all alone. I even worried when I was in college and even after I became a grown-up. I was so afraid that something bad would happen to them. My mom had a bad heart, and eventually, my dad did, too. They are both in Heaven now, but I know that the Lord Jesus is with me even when I am in a lot of pain."

"Wow, that's so sad."

"No, it's really all right. Is there something, in particular, that's making you worry?"

"Well, kind of. I was playing at my neighbor's house, and she has this 8-Ball. You are supposed to ask it yes or no questions, and it answers. She said hers talked if I would ask it questions out loud. So, I did, and it told me all kinds of bad things were going to happen when my parents and I went on vacation."

Best Friends and Bullies

"Corrie, first of all, you need to know that the 8-Ball definitely can't talk. Second, you shouldn't be playing with things like that. Only God knows the future. You need to learn to trust Him and not try to find out answers by experimenting with things like that."

"I know, but I get so afraid sometimes, and I just want to know."

"Corrie, what good would it do for you to know if or when something bad was going to happen to you or your parents? It would keep you from enjoying the present. When you remember that God is in control and that He loves you more than anyone else does, you don't need to worry about what will happen to the people you love. Just concentrate on loving God more than you do anything or anyone else. One way to do that is to read your Bible then think about what God says and what He has promised you."

"I'll try doing that. I was going to ask you something else, but it's really dumb. Thank you for sharing your experience with me."

"Anytime. Let me pray for you before you leave."

Miss Sadie began to pray, "Heavenly Father, thank You that You allowed me to join Sam in ministering to these girls at VBS this week. Thank You for my friendship with Corrie and Lizzie. Father, I ask You that You would help Corrie as she deals with the challenges of NF. Help her to trust You and show others how You can use this trial in her ordinary days so that others see Your work and Your glory in her life. In Jesus' name, Amen."

After they prayed, Corrie walked over to where Lizzie was waiting for her. As she approached her, she said, "Oh, Lizzie, it was so neat. Miss Sadie told me that she worried

Ebenezer

all the time when she was a kid. She said that I really need to read the Bible every day and to think about what it says. I think I'm going to do that."

It was the last day of VBS, and the day before Corrie and her parents would leave for their vacation.

Chapter 11
The Diary

Corrie fell asleep that night with happy thoughts of VBS. It had been so good to meet someone else who understood NF and worried about her parents, as well.

Early the next morning, Corrie and her family left for their vacation to Canada and Lizzie and her family left for a Bible conference. Both girls promised to send postcards to each other even though they would likely see each other before the postcards got there.

The World's Fair was beyond her expectations. She decided to send Lizzie two postcards, one from Niagara Falls and one from the Fair. Had anyone asked her, she would have been hard-pressed to tell what part of her vacation she liked best. She thought Niagara Falls was an incredible sight and she was excited that they got to see it at night with all the lights. But the best part of the trip was sharing with Auntie Maude and Uncle Harry, the fact that she was sure she was saved. At first, it was a little embarrassing because everybody thought that she prayed the salvation prayer at their Bible club, but they were so happy that she really knew for sure that she was saved. To celebrate, they gave her a devotional book, which thrilled her, because she could use it along with the Bible that they had given her when she was five. Corrie and her parents had so much

Best Friends and Bullies

fun in Canada. It was nice to see Auntie Maude and Uncle Harry and, of course, Tippy.

On the way home, Corrie and her parents stopped in Pennsylvania where they spent two nights in the Amish country and watched the horses and buggies go down the road. They even took in a farmer's market, enjoying the fresh produce and the freshly baked goods. Corrie's favorite was the chocolate whoopie pies. All too soon it was over, and they were on their way home.

As they pulled into their driveway, Corrie realized that nothing terrible whatsoever had happened to her parents. Miss Sadie was right; she would never touch that 8-Ball or anything like it again.

Corrie was full of vacation memories when her parents dropped her off at Lizzie's house. Because it was raining, she went into the house instead of sitting under the tree and reading. As usual, Lizzie was still asleep, but Mr. and Mrs. Long sent Corrie upstairs to wake her up.

Lizzie's bedroom door was open so, Corrie walked in. As she gently tapped, Lizzie on the shoulder, she said softly, "Lizzie, your parents wanted me to wake you up."

Lizzie rolled over, sat up, and shouted, "Boo." Then she dissolved into giggles, as she said, "I was only pretending to be asleep. I heard you get out of your car, and I heard you coming up the stairs. I thought it would be fun to scare you again. I had fun on vacation, but I missed you so much. I've never had a friend like you."

Corrie replied, "We had fun, but I missed you, too. Want me to leave so you can get dressed?"

"You can just sit on the bench in the hall. I'll be ready in two shakes."

The Diary

Corrie left the room being careful to shut the door behind her. Soon Lizzie joined her, and they made their way downstairs where Lizzie's parents were sitting down to breakfast. Lizzie and Corrie joined them, and they enjoyed the morning meal together.

As they ate, Mrs. Long asked, "Corrie, how are your aunt and uncle?"

"Oh, they're great. My mom said that they are feeble but vibrant. I asked her what she meant, and she said that their physical health was failing, but they loved Jesus as much as ever, and that makes them appear strong. I want to be like that one day."

"I'm so glad to hear that about them because they were such an encouragement to us in the early years of our ministry here in the city. I know they prayed faithfully for others and I'm sure they still do."

"Oh, and Tippy is great. She really likes it in Canada, but I am pretty sure that she is happy to be anywhere my aunt and uncle are."

"What are you girls going to do today? I think you're stuck in the house, because of the rain."

Lizzie, began, "I don't know . . . "

Corrie interjected, "I know, we can read that old diary we found in the secret panel."

Lizzie responded enthusiastically, "That's a great idea."

Mr. Long said, "I'll be back for lunch, and I want to know what you learned in the diary."

As soon as breakfast was over, the girls started to dash off to Lizzie's room, but Mrs. Long stopped them with the words, "Whoa, Girls! How about some help with the dishes first?"

Lizzie and Corrie both said, "Sure," simultaneously and dove in to help.

As soon as they were done, they went up to Lizzie's room. Corrie insisted that they make Lizzie's bed before they did anything else. Lizzie rolled her eyes but agreed. As soon as the bed was made, Lizzie went to the secret panel and pulled out the old diary. She opened it to the first page and said, "Look! It's sort of an introduction."

Corrie said eagerly, "What does it say?"

"Well, it's written in really fancy cursive writing, but it says 'The Diary of Anna Katherine Parker, age 13,' so, she was a little older than we are, but it says it was written in 1942."

"That's when my parents were kids. I think Daddy was thirteen then. Mom was even younger than we are. Does she say anything about herself?"

"Yeah. Anna wrote, 'I am a student at the Girl's Academy. My parents are Colonel and Mrs. Parker. Father is somewhere in Europe, helping men who are fighting Hitler. He is a chaplain. Mother is very sick, so after school, I come home to take care of her. My older brother went to fight the Japanese after Pearl Harbor was bombed. There are days when I am so afraid. Before he left, father and I talked. He wanted to be sure I knew Jesus as my Savior. We prayed that day, and I know I am God's child, but I still worry.'"

"Hey, Corrie that sounds a little like you except your daddy isn't fighting a war, and your mom isn't sick."

"It does, but does she say any more about worrying?"

The Diary

Lizzie continues, 'One day the chaplain of the school came to speak in chapel. It was a bad day because I was really missing my father and my brother, and I was crying as he spoke. Afterward, he asked to speak to me; I was so afraid, but he was so kind. I told him my worries about the war, my parents and my brother. He prayed with me, but then he told me that I needed to read Psalm 27 and write my thoughts in a journal. This I have done. Once this dreadful war is over, I shall hide it in hopes that in the future another girl who is facing worries may find it and find hope through the words I have written. Our pastor said that our only hope is in the Word of God.'

"Wow! She wrote it and hid it, and we found it," exclaimed Lizzie.

"And I am struggling with worrying. Let's see what Anna says."

"Okay, here goes. She wrote at the top of the page, 'Day 1 Psalm 27:1: The Lord is my light and my Salvation, whom then shall I fear? The Lord is the strength of my life, of whom then shall I be afraid?'

Then she records her thoughts, 'The Lord is my Light – I don't have to be afraid of dark places . . . I should not fill my mind with dark thoughts. I should not read or view dark things that feed these thoughts. I know I have been reading scary books and playing scary games. I will ask God to help me stop doing these things and to read my Bible and think about Him and His mighty power.

The Lord is my Salvation – since Jesus is my Savior, I am perfectly safe now and in eternity . . . that means when I die I will go to that awesome place called Heaven. I really need to stop worrying about Mother, Father, and Bobby, because even if something terrible happens to them, I know they will be in Heaven with Jesus, because they, too, have believed in Jesus as their Savior.

The Lord is my strength or my fortress – another word for this is stronghold. Many years ago – even in Bible times, kings and queens would fight battles. They would wall themselves into their castles – it was their place of safety. The LORD is our place of safety – no one can break through that stronghold. With the LORD as my Stronghold, I am perfectly safe. I can stop worrying about my family.'

"Wow," Corrie said, "She really had faith and understood her Bible. That makes me so ashamed. I mean, her father and her brother were fighting a war. Her mother had heart disease. I worry that my parents might get into a wreck. What else does she say?"

Lizzie read on, 'Day 2 – Psalm 27:2: When the wicked, even mine enemies and my foes, came upon me to eat up my flesh, they stumbled and fell. Sometimes people scare me. I am terrified of Hitler and what might happen in Europe. Here in America, some people really scare me. There are those mean boys I see every day on the way to school who tell me I am going to be an orphan girl because my parents are going to die – mother of her illness and father in the war. The rich girls at school make fun of my clothes because they are hand-me-downs. I try not to let other people know, but I really can't run and jump, because my legs look funny from polio and don't work right. I think everyone laughs when I try to do anything. Sometimes I hate them, and I hate myself. Sometimes I think mother would not be sick if I had been a better daughter. Some people have even asked if my birth hurt my mother's heart. I'm afraid to ask

The Diary

her because I don't know what the answer will be. When I asked Pastor Andrews, he said that all of those people and thoughts are like enemies and the LORD is our Light, our Salvation, and our Stronghold, and it says that He wants to help me stand strong against them.'

Corrie said, "That is so cool. She said that God really cares when thoughts and words hurt us, and He wants us to be strong enough to stand against them. Isn't that amazing? It's like she knew someday a girl would find her dairy and know how she would feel. There will always be annoying boys, mean girls, and physical limitations, but God will help me stand against them by not letting me worry about them or make me unhappy."

Lizzie looked at the clock on the wall and noted, "Maybe we should put it away for now. We have an hour before lunch, and I think we can go outside for a few minutes. I think it's stopped raining."

Corrie answered, "Okay, but I can't wait to see what else Anna Katherine has to say. Until tomorrow then."

Chapter 12
Not That!

That evening as the Cushman family sat down to supper, Corrie was full of excitement about the diary she and Lizzie had found. She was talking so much that she was neglecting her food.

"It was written by a girl back when you and Daddy were kids. She was thirteen. Her father was fighting Hitler, and her brother was fighting the Japanese during the war. She said her mother was really sick with a bad heart. Because she was so worried, somebody told her to read Psalm 27 and start writing about it. Lizzie and I read through the first two verses of Psalm 27 ourselves today. WOW! I am so excited; I can't wait to see what else she says."

Her mother replied, "That sounds really interesting. I know you are excited to see what happens. I guess you plan on doing that tomorrow."

"We do. Why is something wrong?"

"You have an appointment with Dr. Keener tomorrow. He wants to check on the progress you're making with the brace."

"Oh, you mean old Goofball? I told you he goofs up everything. Now Lizzie and I may not get to read the diary at all tomorrow. At least he didn't ruin our vacation."

Best Friends and Bullies

Mr. and Mrs. Cushman looked at their daughter holding back smiles. Corrie caught the look and quickly said, "Well, you know what I mean."

Mr. Cushman looked at his daughter with affection and said, "I know it hasn't been easy, and you've done well for the most part. Dr. Keener just wants to check your progress and see if anything else can be done."

"Like what?"

"Let's wait and see what he says. In fact, tomorrow I'm going along. I have some questions of my own for Dr. Keener."

"Can we stop and buy doughnuts on our way back to Lizzie's house?"

"I don't see why not. Did I ever tell you that the doughnut shop was built when I was a little boy? In fact, I actually saw them lay the first brick and watched the building go up as I went to and from school. You had better believe that I got one of the first doughnuts off the line."

"Were they as good back then as they are now?"

"Better and cheaper. I could buy two for five cents."

"That's so cool. We pay five cents for one now and seven cents if they put chocolate icing on it. Those are the best."

The rest of the evening passed without further discussion of the upcoming doctor's appointment, but as a diversion, Corrie's parents engaged her in a game of Parcheesi. Mr. Cushman had been a Parcheesi champ as a boy, and he had retained his skill, so he quickly took first place. Mrs. Cushman was a comfortable second, leaving Corrie in third place, but it didn't matter to her. It just felt good to be together.

Not That!

The next morning the Cushmans left and went to the doctor. For some reason, Corrie was more apprehensive than usual. Since her father was going with them, it made her think that the visit was more than just a check-up on her and Goofball. She did her best not to let her parents see how worried she was; however, she did not realize how concerned they were. She took her book just in case there was a long wait. They arrived at Dr. Keener's office, checked in, and had a seat. Corrie opened her book, but before she could read a page, the nurse called them back. As before, Corrie was invited to take a seat on the doctor's table. Her parents sat in the other available chairs in the room. Dr. Keener came in and shook hands with everyone. Then, he asked, "What can I do for you today?"

Mr. Cushman took the lead and said, "We are concerned about how Corrie is doing. She is in a lot of discomfort. We were wondering if you have anything else to offer?"

Dr. Keener looked at Corrie and asked, "How do you think things are going? How are you feeling?"

Corrie scrunched up her face and answered, "Well, Goofball, that's what I named my brace, is really uncomfortable. There are days when my back and head really hurt. I don't want people to know, because they will think I am a big baby. It's hard to run and jump; at least I'm not in school where we have to play games."

Dr. Keener noted what she said and asked her to climb down from the table. He told Mrs. Cushman to remove Goofball since he thought that would be more comfortable for Corrie and would better allow him to assess her progress. Then he had Corrie go through the same movements as before.

Best Friends and Bullies

When he had finished, he looked at the Cushmans and said, "I have to admit that I can tell very little difference. Of course, it is a little too soon to make an evaluation. I do think that we should add some additional things to strengthen those stubborn muscles."

Mrs. Cushman looked at him and asked, "What do you suggest? You are aware that we are opposed to medicine except for an occasional pain reliever."

"Nothing like that. I would like to suggest that Corrie take swimming lessons for the rest of the summer and then move to physical therapy for the fall and winter months."

A look of panic passed over Corrie's face as she shook her head at her parents. Her dad spoke up quickly, "That may be a solution, but Corrie has had limited exposure to water and is not all that comfortable in the water."

The doctor continued, "I can recommend a swimming teacher who can help her with the necessary movements to strengthen her muscles and help her to get over her fear of the water. I realize that you can't decide right now without talking it over. Why don't you take a few days to think about it?"

"Thank you for understanding, Doctor. We will discuss it and get back to you in the next few days."

The Cushmans left the office and got into their car. Corrie spoke first, "Can we talk about this at supper this evening?"

Her parents agreed to delay the conversation until supper. Then the conversation turned to doughnuts. Corrie chose to take four chocolate-iced doughnuts that she could share with Lizzie and her parents. She was eager to get to the Longs so that she and Lizzie could continue reading in the diary.

Not That!

When the Cushmans arrived at the Longs, Corrie climbed out of the car and walked to their house. She knocked on the door and was immediately greeted by Lizzie.

"What did the doctor say?"

"Nothing much, but there are some things Mom, Daddy, and I have to talk about this evening. When we figure it out, I can tell you. Do you want a doughnut?"

"Don't tell me. All you had for breakfast was a graham cracker and some juice."

"How'd you know?"

"Lucky guess. You want some milk with the doughnuts?"

"If you do."

"Are you always so agreeable?"

"It depends. I brought doughnuts for your parents, too."

"Cool. They'll like that."

The girls enjoyed their doughnuts and milk. As they ate, Corrie shared the story of her dad and the doughnut shop. When they were finished, Corrie asked, "Can we read more of the diary today?"

"I hoped you would want to."

The two girls went up to Lizzie's room and retrieved the diary from her closet. Then, they sat together on Lizzie's bed and lost themselves in the happenings of 1942.

Lizzie began to read, 'Day 3 Psalm 27:3: Though an host should encamp against me, my heart shall not fear; though war should rise against me in this I will be confident.'

"Let's see what Anna says about this:" 'Sometimes other children are mean to me and they call me names. I have trouble with the stuff that comes into my mind like what if my father and brother get killed fighting this war or what if my mother dies from the heart disease she has or why do the children at school call me names when I try to run and play their games? Even if it seems like an army of bullies is coming after me . . . Even if bad and scary thoughts are coming at me like arrows, I can stand strong. Why? The Lord is my LIGHT . . . my SALVATION . . . and He is my STRONGHOLD surrounding me to keep me safe.'

Lizzie stopped there, looked at Corrie, and asked, "What do you think?"

"She really knows how to trust God. I wish I could learn how to do that. Can we read the next day, too?"

"I was hoping you would want to," Lizzie replied, "Let's see," 'Day 4 Psalm 27:4 says: One thing have I desired of the Lord, that will I seek after; that I may dwell in the house of the Lord all the days of my life, to behold the beauty of the Lord, and to enquire in his temple.'

"Anna writes about that as well. I keep thinking about what I want more than anything, like one of those 57-game Carrom boards, or a new dress and more Nancy Drew books, but I know there is something God wants for me. This gift from Him will help me not to be afraid if I say yes to what He wants for me. That is for me to stay close to Him all the days of my life. The Bible calls it 'staying in His temple. I know it doesn't mean that I have to be in church all the time, but it does mean that I need to read my Bible and pray every day so that God and I can have a relationship. That relationship will be great protection against all those bad and scary thoughts. I do want God as my friend. I am so glad I have trusted Jesus as my Savior – I want to keep on trusting Him as my forever friend."

Not That!

Corrie said, "I really like that thought of God being my forever friend. I know Jesus is my Savior, but I want Him to be my friend, too. That way, when people are mean to me, or I get anxious about Mom and Daddy, I can talk to Him. I'm going to start reading my Bible every day and write a journal just like Anna Katherine's."

"I will too. Maybe we can read the same thing and then meet and discuss our journals."

"Yeah, let's do that. I can't wait until tomorrow when we get to read more about Anna Katherine."

The day passed as the girls found various ways to occupy themselves. Soon Corrie's parents picked her up and headed home. As they sat down to supper, she knew it was time for the dreaded conversation. She decided to begin, "Mom, Daddy, what was Dr. Keener talking about this morning?"

Mr. Cushman chose to reply, "He thinks that some form of physical therapy or swimming lessons will help you with your pain and strengthen your muscles."

Corrie wrinkled her nose and said, "I'm afraid of water since that boy we called old pest tried to dunk me at that motel. I don't think I can put my head in the water and physical therapy sounds like it will really hurt."

Mr. Cushman suppressed a smile as he responded, "I know, but I think that moving in the water will really help you. It's a little easier moving in the water than moving on land. I really would like for you to learn to swim. Neither your mother nor I can swim very well."

"Well, I guess I could try if you really want me to. Who would teach me?"

Best Friends and Bullies

"The doctor recommended a young man he knew was qualified to give swimming lessons that would be able to help you not only get over your fear of the water, but also help you with exercises that would strengthen the muscles in your body. His family has a backyard pool, and we can make arrangements for him to teach you to swim, too."

Corrie interrupted, as she said, "A pool at his house? That is so cool!"

"Yes, it is, but what do you think about the swimming lessons?"

"I guess we can try them, but how would I get there? I really don't want to do it alone."

"We do have a plan. We thought about asking Mr. Long to take you. In exchange, we would pay for lessons for Lizzie. That way, you wouldn't be alone."

"I'll try it if you really want me to. And thank you! Thank you for inviting Lizzie to go with me."

"You are so welcome. We know this whole thing has been difficult for you, and we want to make things as pleasant as we can. We'll set up the lessons. I really think you and Lizzie will enjoy them. It will give you a break from that dusty old diary you are so obsessed with. By the way, what's Anna Katherine up to today?"

"Basically, she wrote about wanting God more than anything. Lizzie and I have decided to start reading the Bible and writing a journal just like Anna Katherine did. I think that will be exciting."

"That will be good for you," her dad said. "It's important that you read God's Word. I know you have been using the devotional that Auntie Maude gave you, but I think this approach will also be good for you. You know you can talk things over with Mom or me anytime.

Not That!

"Corrie smiled and hugged her father, as she said, "Thanks, Daddy I love you!"

The next morning, Corrie's parents told her that arrangements had been made for the swimming lessons. She and Lizzie would start the next day and would go three days each week. Corrie smiled, because she knew anytime Lizzie was involved, things would be fun.

When they arrived at the Longs the following day, Lizzie was up and dressed. Lizzie was beyond excited as she exclaimed, "I am so excited about swimming or whatever it is we will be doing, I thought I had better practice getting up and dressed earlier than I have been."

"You're crazy, Lizzie, but I like you anyway."

"Come on, let's eat breakfast and then read more about Anna Katherine."

The girls hastily devoured the cereal that Mrs. Long put in front of them, but before they could disappear into Lizzie's room, she suggested that they take a walk, because they needed the sunshine. They reluctantly agreed and went outside. As they walked, Corrie asked Lizzie, "I've been meaning to ask you something. What happened to Dall when you moved? Is he okay?"

"Oh, Dall is fine. We gave him to some people in our church who live in the country. Now he can roam around their land, and he doesn't have to stay chained to the doghouse. I think he's a lot happier."

"Oh, I thought something bad had happened to him. I'm glad he's okay and happy."

The girls continued their walk around the outer perimeters of the house and church. When they felt they had been outside long enough, they went inside and made their way to Lizzie's room where they took the diary from its hiding place.

Lizzie began to read: 'Day 5 Psalm 27:5: For in the day of trouble he will keep me safe in his dwelling; he will hide me in the shelter of his sacred tent and set me high upon a rock.'

"Wow! That's a cool verse even on its own. Let's see what Anna Katherine thought about it. She wrote," – 'I really like this. When I stay close to God by reading my Bible and praying, I can trust Him to protect me. When I am afraid, He can shield me from danger. I asked our pastor about this, and he said that it is like being taken to the safest place in the middle of the army – the general's tent and nobody messes with him! He said that God wants us to know how far He goes to keep us safe.'

Corrie stopped her and said, "I think that must have meant a lot to her with her father and brother off fighting that war. I think she could just see that in her mind and knew that God was stronger than any general."

Lizzie added, "I like that, too. It shows how much God loves me."

Lizzie continued reading, 'David, the Psalmist draws a picture of a being placed high on a rock – where nothing can get to me without His permission. I think of it like this – where do I put my most prized possessions – my most favorite toys or my most important books? I put them on a high shelf or lock them in a closet so that our dog, Sammy, can't chew them up or the little kids who visit can't mess with them. Pastor says that because I know the Lord Jesus as my Savior – I am God's prized possession, and He will keep me safe. I could say the same thing about my father and my brother. It's like they've been put on the very

Not That!

highest shelf – out of the reach of anyone who could hurt them – not even the Germans or the Japanese can unless God lets them. And I know that if they do die, they will be safe forever with God in Heaven.'

Lizzie exclaimed, "Wow, she really seems to understand what it means to trust God."

Corrie pondered, "I wonder how she knows so much about trusting God. I really think it comes from her reading and studying the Bible so much. Maybe we need to learn to do that. It would sure help with these swimming lessons and always worrying about Mom. I am God's prized possession. I need to think about that every day. Lizzie, please help me remember that."

Chapter 13
Water Therapy

As Corrie got her things together that evening, her mother reminded her to get her bathing suit, a towel, and an extra change of clothes. Even though her parents tried to reassure her, Corrie's mother noticed that her daughter was pretty nervous.

"Corrie, what's wrong?"

Corrie proceeded to express her concerns, "I'm just afraid. What if I mess up; what if the teacher tries to push me underwater; what if I'm no good?"

"You will be fine, sweetheart. Ben is a teacher, and teachers don't intentionally hurt their students or at least they shouldn't. If you have any problems, you need to tell Daddy or me."

"Okay. I will."

The next day, Corrie arrived at Lizzie's house. She had her swimsuit on under her clothes, and she carried a clean set of clothes in her backpack. They each ate a piece of peanut butter toast for breakfast, because Mrs. Long said they needed the protein to perform well in the water. Mr. Long drove the girls to Ben's house just before 10:00 that morning with the promise to pick them up around 11:00.

Best Friends and Bullies

Ben was waiting for the girls in the front yard of his house. His hair was blonde, and his skin deeply tan. He smiled as he welcomed the girls, "Good morning! My name is Ben, but I guess you already know that. And I bet your names are Lizzie and Corrie. Come on, I'll walk you around to the pool, and we'll get started."

As they walked, Ben began to ask questions, "Can either of you swim?" Lizzie said that she could, but Corrie simply shook her head.

Ben replied, "That's no problem. I spoke with your dad, and he said that the doctor was mainly interested in water exercises to strengthen your back and other muscles. I am studying to be a physical therapist, so I thought we would start with water exercises and games. That will allow you to get more comfortable in the water."

For the next hour, he led them through water jumping jacks, knee lifts, walking races from one end of the shallow end to the other, and activities with a ball. He ended by challenging the girls to a splashing contest. Of course, he won, and both girls were thoroughly drenched, but much of the tension had left Corrie's face as she emerged from the pool. She felt as though she had overcome a huge hurdle. After the lesson, the girls relaxed on lounge chairs to dry off. Then they slipped into their outer clothes to cover their suits. As they waited for Mr. Long, Corrie turned to Lizzie and said, "I think I can do this."

Lizzie smiled and said, "I never had a doubt."

After lunch, as the girls were resting in Lizzie's room, their thoughts turned again to the diary hidden in the secret compartment. Corrie asked, "Lizzie, can I go get the diary?"

Lizzie replied, "Sure, go ahead."

Water Therapy

Corrie retrieved the diary and gave it to Lizzie who began reading, 'Day 4 Psalm 27:6-8: And now shall my head be lifted up above mine enemies round about me: therefore, will I offer in his tabernacle sacrifices of joy; I will sing, yea, I will sing praises to the LORD. Hear O LORD, when I cry with my voice: Have mercy also upon me and answer me. When thou saidst, seek ye my face; my heart said unto thee, thy face LORD, I will seek.'

"Let's see what she said about these verses. She wrote," 'When I am sure of God's deliverance and protection from danger for myself and for my family, I can praise Him. I do know that protection may also mean going home to Heaven, and that's the absolute best. I may not feel like smiling because I am going through a hard time, or I'm sad. Even when I am going through those hard times, I will remember to sing praises, because that reminds people how great God is and that He is a God who deserves their trust as well.'

"She continued writing about the next verse, I guess." 'God really does hear us when we pray, but sometimes I think we need reminders like string ties around our fingers, or bookmarks in our Bibles. This verse is a good reminder that God wants to hear from me. The word pray means to have a conversation with God.

It's more than asking for stuff – it's thanking God for what He has done for me. It's giving praise to His name, just because He's a great and wonderful God. It's telling Him I'm sorry for the wrong things I've done. And yes, it's asking for things I need and want, but with an attitude of being willing to accept His answers, even if it is no or wait awhile.'

Corrie interrupted, "I like that. Sometimes when I've

119

messed up, I want to run away from God, but I know He still sees me. He wants me to come to Him and ask for forgiveness."

Lizzie responded, "And did you see that she said sometimes God answers prayer with yes, no or wait a while? Remember how you prayed the NF would go away or you wouldn't have to wear Goofball, but God said no to that prayer. It wasn't like He didn't listen. I guess He wants you to use it to help people know how great He is and to help people see that you love Him no matter what."

"Let's see what else she says:" 'You want me to come to You; You want me to share my thoughts with You . . . my secrets . . . what I'm thinking . . . what makes me happy . . . what makes me sad . . . what I'm worried about. That's a big part of prayer.'

Corrie said, "Wow! That's amazing that God wants to hear from me. I guess I have to do a better job of talking to Him and really sharing my thoughts – about Goofball, my parents, and Robin. He really does care about everything."

Lizzie turned back to the diary, "Oh look, Verse 9 is missing, but then she seems to write her thoughts about some things going on with the war.

'People in our neighborhood are sad today. Ever since this awful war began and men went to fight the Germans and Japanese, families flew flags with blue stars. If someone in their family were killed, they would fly a flag with a gold star. Today, two families found out their sons had been killed in the fighting in Europe and so they were given flags with gold stars. Mother flies a blue flag for my brother, and Granny flies a blue flag for my Father. I am so afraid that our flags will turn to gold before this horrid war

Water Therapy

is over. Then today I was reading Psalm 27:10, When my father and mother forsake me, the Lord will take me up. At first, I didn't understand the forsaking part, but since it was Sunday, I asked Pastor Allsburg what it meant. He told me that some people believe that forsake can mean that they've gone on before – like they've gone to Heaven ahead of us. When that happens, and we are sad because they are gone, then God is there to help them. Children who lose their daddies or mommies in this war aren't really alone if they know Jesus, because they have a Father in Heaven who is always with them. He also told me that earlier in the Depression, some men would give up and walk away from their families. Their children really were forsaken, but God is there to take care of them, and He is their Father if they know Jesus. That's why it's so important that everyone knows Jesus as Savior so that they can really know that they have a Father in Heaven. I think the coolest thing is that He is our Light, our Salvation, and our Stronghold. He is our perfect place of protection and our forever friend. We know that nothing can change that relationship.'

Corrie paused and then looked at Lizzie as she said, "I really like Anna's words that even if our mommies or daddies die, we will never be without a Father. I'm so glad that I have trusted Jesus as my Savior and that God is my Father – no matter what happens."

Lizzie nodded her head in agreement and noted, "Anna Katherine must have been a special girl. I wonder if her father and brother came home from the war. I wonder what happened to her. I guess it's a mystery that we'll never solve. I sure am glad we found her diary. It's been fun reading it, and we really learned a lot about trusting God."

Chapter 14
Back to School

The summer soon came to an end. During the last days of summer, the girls enjoyed reading and playing their made-up games. Corrie's parents took them on a day trip to see a replica of an old western town, complete with a railroad. Mrs. Cushman managed to attend a few of the sessions with Ben and observe the water therapy. He gave suggestions regarding what could be done in the bathtub and on the bed once school started, and the sessions with him ended.

Lizzie and Corrie were delighted to learn that once again, they would be in the same class and that their teacher would be Mrs. Sipp. She even sent out a letter to each student in her class explaining what to expect in the coming year. Corrie was at Lizzie's house the day Lizzie received her letter. They read it together, knowing that Corrie would have a similar letter in her mailbox.

Dear Lizzie,

Welcome to Mrs. Sipp's fifth-grade classroom. I am looking forward to this year and to meeting you. I anticipate having a great year. We will be studying exciting topics in each subject area. Perhaps the most significant change you will see is that in addition to our basal reader, we will be exploring a novel each quarter. The first book we will be reading is *The Lion, the Witch, and the Wardrobe*. It is a work of fantasy, but I think you will enjoy it. If you have not already read it, please do not begin it before the beginning of the semester. Other subject areas will give us the opportunity for great learning experiences. Each student will be completing a science project in the fall and a history project in the spring. I hope you can attend the Meet the Teacher special PTA meeting on August 20 from 6:30 to 8:30. I have attached a list of supplies I would like for each of you to have before the beginning of school. Have a great rest of the summer. Hope to see you on August 20.

Sincerely,

Mrs. Sipp

As Lizzie completed reading the letter, Corrie looked at her and asked, "Well, what do you think?"

"She sounds really nice. I think this is going to be a cool year. I just wish she hadn't said not to start the book."

"I know, but we have to be patient. I guess Mrs. Sipp wants the class to stay together."

"I know, but still . . ."

"Hey, I have an idea. Let's go play hide and seek in the church."

"I don't think so. You would definitely win, and I would get lost."

"Well, we could go look around. You've never seen the balcony and the bell tower."

Back to School

"Is it okay?"

"Corrie, I keep telling you – you worry too much. It's fine. We might even ring the bell."

"Won't we get in trouble?'

Lizzie sighed and rolled her eyes. After that, Corrie stopped asking questions and followed Lizzie's lead. The two girls walked across the yard to the church. The door they used opened directly into Mr. Long's office. Lizzie knocked with her secret knock, just in case, someone was in the office with her father. If there was no response, she knew not to enter. On this particular day, Mr. Long called out, "Come in, girls!"

As they walked through the door, Lizzie looked at him and said, "Hi, Daddy! Is it all right if Corrie and I look around? She wants to see the balcony and the bell since her church doesn't have one."

"I think that would be all right. Just be very careful and don't fall. Are you by any chance thinking of ringing the bell?"

"That would be nice. I think Corrie would really like to ring it. You know Mr. Hampton lets me help him ring it some Sundays."

Mr. Long leaned back in his chair and rubbed his chin before answering his daughter. He asked, "What time is it?"

Lizzie looked at the clock on the wall and replied, "It's about 1:30."

He said, "I'll tell you what. Can you wait until 2:00 and each of you can ring it once to sound the hour? That way we won't alarm the neighbors. Years ago, the church used to sound the hour. The old-timers in our community will remember that. By waiting until 2:00, people will just assume that's what we're doing."

"Cool! Thank you, Daddy!"

"Yes, thank you, Mr. Long!"

The girls left his study giddy with excitement. They walked to the back of the church sanctuary, which was a bit eerie since it was empty. The steps to the balcony were located in the foyer. They carefully climbed the steps. Once they were there, they had fun looking over the edge and wandering around the pews.

Corrie exclaimed, "This is neat! If my church had a balcony, I would never sit anywhere else."

Lizzie agreed, "Yeah, it is pretty neat. What time does your watch say?"

"It's about 1:52."

"Then we had better start-up to the bell tower."

The two girls carefully climbed the narrow, steep stairway. Corrie stopped to rest once. Lizzie was waiting for her when she arrived at the top. The two girls walked over to the rope, which was hanging down from the bell. Lizzie reached out and gave it a tug. Corrie's eyes were huge, as she walked over and took her turn. She smiled as she heard the result of her own tugging of the rope. Lizzie silenced it as she had been shown. Then the girls left and made their way down the narrow staircase. As they stepped into the balcony, Corrie asked, "Can we stop for a rest?"

"Sure, I guess those steps are pretty daunting."

"Yeah, and old Goofball doesn't help matters any. I'm sorry. I know I complain a lot. I should ask the Lord to help me with that."

Back to School

"It's okay. I know you hurt and tire easily. Let's just sit here and look at the stained-glass windows. Don't you love the patterns?"

"Yeah, they are pretty cool. Our windows are just beige."

After looking at the windows from their high vantage point, the girls discussed the patterns and planned to draw similar patterns once they got back to the house. Corrie smiled as she said, "I don't think even I can mess that up."

As they descended the stairs and walked back through Mr. Long's office, he looked up and asked, "How was the bell ringing?"

Corrie's eyes lit up with joy, "Oh, it was great fun! Thank you for letting us ring it!"

The afternoon passed quickly as the girls worked on their stained-glass window creations. This would be their last afternoon of the summer together before school started.

When Corrie arrived home with her parents, she ran to the mailbox to see if her letter from Mrs. Sipp was there. It was, and she and her parents read it together. Her mother promised that they would go and get the required supplies when they shopped for school clothes.

That evening as the family ate supper, Corrie excitedly told her parents about ringing the bell. They were happy to have their daughter in such good spirits.

Chapter 15
Girls Club

As they discussed the beginning of school, her parents reminded Corrie about the Girls Club starting at their church on the Friday evening after Labor Day.

Corrie's eyes lit up as she began to ask questions, "What was the name of the group?"

Mrs. Cushman answered, "We're calling it Girls for Christ. It's a lot like Girl Scouts in that you will work to earn badges, but there will be Bible studies and more of a Christian focus."

"Can Lizzie come, too?"

"As long as it's okay with her parents. You might want to ask some of the girls in the neighborhood as well."

"I guess I can. I'm pretty sure Maggie would really like it."

"Well, when we get the details in place, you can ask Lizzie, Maggie, and the others."

"That sounds good to me."

"Now, there is one other thing we need to discuss. I will be starting to work full time the Tuesday after Labor Day. That's the day Bessie starts working for us. She will be here next Friday for me to show her around. After that, she will come on the bus before we leave for work and leave as soon as we get home. She will always be here when you get home from school."

"Will she help me make a snack?"

"If you want her to or I'm sure she would be happy to make it for you."

"Will she make supper for us?"

"That's the plan."

"What if we don't like what she cooks?"

"She'll make what we ask her to and the way we want it made."

"I like your cooking."

"I know you do, but we'll be fine. You need to be patient as she learns what we want and like."

"I'll try. I really will."

"I know."

"I'm so thankful this is working out."

Corrie and her mother went on the promised shopping trip for the required supplies, a new lunch box, and a couple of new outfits. On Sunday, the official announcement about Girls for Christ was made at church. It sounded even better than Corrie had imagined – working on badges, studying the Bible, and having fun with friends. Corrie was over the moon to learn that Miss Sadie would be attending their church. She would also be the adult leader for her age group. The only thing that would make it better would be for Lizzie to be able to come. She could hardly wait to ask her.

On the appointed Monday evening, the Cushmans and the Longs met at the Cushman's house and walked to the school together. Both Lizzie and Corrie knew that they were going to love fifth grade. The bulletin boards

Girls Club

and wall hangings popped with enthusiasm. While the parents were there, Mrs. Sipp explained the expectations for her classroom, including the two required projects. The science project was in the fall. Students could choose from the following topics: the human body, weather, or outer space. For the spring project, students could do a mapping project or something associated with the Colonial Days of the United States. After the announcements and a time of fellowship and refreshments, the Longs and the Cushmans began their walk home.

As they walked, Mrs. Cushman and Mrs. Long chatted together. Corrie and Lizzie followed close behind, whispering about the prospect of starting school the next morning. They wanted to dress alike and decided on khaki skirts and navy polo shirts. Then they fell silent and listened to their mothers' conversation. Finally, Corrie heard her mother ask the question she had been longing to ask. "Margaret, our church is starting a Girls Club. It is very similar to Girl Scouts, but it has a strong Christian emphasis. They will meet on Friday evenings. Would you be willing for Lizzie to attend?"

"I think that sounds delightful. I'm sure Lizzie would enjoy it. Why don't you have Corrie invite her?"

Unbeknownst to their mothers, the girls had been following the conversation. Lizzie whispered, "I sure would like to go with you. It sounds like fun."

"Okay, but I need to wait for Mom to tell me I can ask you. She doesn't like it when I listen in."

Lizzie rolled her eyes but kept quiet.

When they got home, Mrs. Cushman told Corrie, "Mrs. Long said that it would be all right to invite Lizzie to the Girls

Best Friends and Bullies

Club. Have you asked any of the girls in the neighborhood?"

"I did, but Maggie is the only one who wanted to go right now. I think the others are waiting to see how it goes. Is it okay if I tell Lizzie when we walk to school tomorrow?"

Mrs. Cushman consented to that plan and then suggested that Corrie get ready for bed so that she would have a few minutes to read before she turned her light out. Corrie did as her mother suggested then hung her clothes for the following day on the closet knob.

Morning came early, but Corrie rose willingly. Her mother came in to help her with Goofball and suggested that she eat a hot breakfast for this first day of school. Corrie wrinkled her nose but knew this was important to her mother and asked for French toast because she knew it was her mother's favorite breakfast. Corrie appeared in the kitchen dressed for school and breathed in the aroma of the freshly made breakfast. After a prayer of blessing on the food, they began to eat together. As a special treat, they had hot tea in the bunny cups given to Corrie by Auntie Maude. When breakfast was over, Corrie went to her room to finish getting ready. She grabbed her backpack loaded with school supplies, walked to the kitchen, and grabbed her lunch box. She started to open it, but her mother stopped her with the words, "Don't open it. It's a surprise for lunch."

Corrie gave her mother a grin and kiss and then walked out the door to meet Lizzie who was waiting at the end of the sidewalk. The two girls walked to school, chatting about the upcoming year. They each knew that it would hold challenges, but they were equally as sure it would bring joys. Corrie still had Goofball to contend with, and they knew that Robin would be in their class and would continue to be a nemesis, particularly to Corrie, but their goal was to make her a friend rather than an enemy. With this resolve, they walked into their classroom together. They stored their lunches in the cloakroom and went to find their seats.

As they had anticipated, Robin was there ready to pounce on Corrie's weakness. She opened her mouth to ask, "Well, Corrie, did the summer make you any less clumsy?"

At that moment, Corrie tripped but managed to keep from falling by grabbing on to the desk beside her. Mrs. Sipp walked over and greeted the three girls with a cheery, "Good morning." Then they hastily found their seats.

At lunch, Corrie was pleasantly surprised to have a Lebanon bologna sandwich in her lunch box, along with her favorite chips, a side of pickles and a special dessert. She purchased milk in the cafeteria and sat down to an enjoyable lunch. The rest of the day passed quickly, and soon it was time to go home. The assignment for that night was to read the first chapter in *The Lion the Witch and the Wardrobe* and answer a question in their response journal. The following morning, they would exchange journals and answer a classmate. They would also be introduced to vocabulary words from the book.

On Friday morning, Bessie was at the house before Corrie left for school. Her appearance made Corrie realize that her mother was starting to work soon, but she managed to smile and be polite. As she left, she gave her mother her usual kiss before she walked out the door. School seemed to drag that day because Corrie was excited about the first meeting of the Girls Club.

That evening Corrie accompanied by Lizzie and Maggie joined around 40 other girls aged 8-15 at the church for the opening meeting of the Girls Club. After a brief opening assembly, the girls divided into groups by age. The 10 - 11-year olds were in a group together with Miss Sadie as their leader. They were given their badge books and instructed to look through their books and find a badge they were interested in working on as a group. They would also be free to work on badges individually. The group decided to work on a community service badge and set about planning their work to complete the requirements.

Corrie and Lizzie conspired together to work on the Kitchen Skills badge. One of the requirements was to make cookies. They asked Miss Sadie if they could bring the snack the next week to help fulfill this requirement. When she said, "Yes," they decided to make the cookies the following Thursday at Corrie's house as long as their parents said it was okay.

When Corrie got home that evening, she asked her mother, "May Lizzie and I make cookies for Girls Club next week. It will help us get our Kitchen Skills badge."

"Is that all you have to do?"

"No, there are several requirements. We need to set the table for a week. Learn how to set a fancy table and draw a picture of it. Then we have to plan a week's worth of suppers using the different food groups. There are one or two other things, but we thought we would start with the cookies and setting the table next week."

"I think that making cookies would be fine and since you usually set the table anyway, that is taken care of. You don't by any chance have to do the dishes?"

"I think so. Maybe you could teach me how to load and unload the dishwasher."

Girls Club

"I think that can be arranged. Now, what kind of cookies do you want to make? We need to be sure we have the ingredients that you need."

"Lizzie said I could pick since we are making them here. What about cowboy cookies? I've watched you or Aunt Sally make them tons of times."

"Well, you are familiar with those and Bessie will be here if you need help. But let her put them in and out of the oven."

"Okay, we can do that."

The next Thursday, the girls met in the kitchen at Corrie's house. Bessie helped them get the ingredients together and even helped them stir when the batter got too thick. And, of course, she pulled them in and out of the oven. The girls cleaned up their mess and washed the dishes so that the kitchen was in good order. When the cookies were cool, they packed them in boxes, but not before the girls and Bessie taste-tested them and proclaimed them delicious. The girls thanked Bessie profusely for her help, saying they could not have done it without her. Corrie also put a few out for dessert for her parents. After setting the table, the girls sat down to relax until suppertime. Corrie's parents were just as happy with the cookies as Bessie had been. Now if only their friends liked them as much as the adults had said they did.

Friday afternoon, Corrie went home with Lizzie for supper. Supper was spaghetti, and during the meal, Lizzie got a gleam in her eye that let Corrie know something was about to happen. As Lizzie opened her mouth to sing the worm song, her mother gave her a stern glance, and Lizzie resumed eating her meal.

Best Friends and Bullies

After the meal, the girls helped Mrs. Long clean the kitchen, while Mr. Long walked over to his study at the church to retrieve a few books. When the kitchen was in order, the girls took a few minutes to compare notes on their Kitchen Skills badge. They still had a few things to do but knew they would have plenty of time to finish by the awards ceremony the third week in November.

Soon it was time to go, but Lizzie wanted to run over to the church to tell her dad goodbye. Corrie slipped out behind her, tiptoeing. As Lizzie stepped into the office, Corrie hid behind a protruding column. She listened and watched for Lizzie's exit since she had left the door open. Lizzie soon stepped through the door and on to the small sidewalk and then took a couple of steps into the yard. Corrie crept up behind her, tapped her shoulder, and roared loudly. Lizzie screamed and ran for the car. Corrie stopped, horrified at how badly she had scared her friend. As she reached the car, she heard Lizzie explaining to her mother what had frightened her so badly.

When Corrie appeared, she immediately said, "I am so sorry. I was just trying to have fun with you as you do with me."

Lizzie gave her a weak smile as she said, "It's okay. I'll stop scaring you now that I know how it feels."

Chapter 16
Fall Doings

Monday morning came in crisp and refreshing. As Corrie emerged from her room and sat down at the table for breakfast, her dad remarked, "There's a taste of fall in the air."

Corrie responded, "It is cool. I might wear slacks today. I think they would look better with tennis shoes and socks. I'll still wear a short-sleeved shirt since it might get hot this afternoon."

Mrs. Cushman joined the conversation, "I think that would be fine. I can help you tie your shoes if you like when I help with Goofball."

"That would be good. Thanks. Can I have Cheerios for breakfast?"

"Sure. I'll pour some grape juice, too."

Corrie ate quickly and went back to her room to get ready. Her mother came to assist where needed and put her hair in pigtails. Then they walked together to the kitchen where her mother helped her prepare her lunch, consisting of a ham sandwich with just a smidge of mustard, a few chips, and two cookies. She planned to buy her drink in the school cafeteria. It felt good to be gaining a little independence.

Best Friends and Bullies

As she closed her lunchbox Lizzie, appeared at the door. As they walked to school, they talked about how to approach Robin since she didn't seem to like either of them.

"Isn't today free play day? Why don't we see if she wants to play four square with us? We can see if Wendy wants to play, too. That would make four of us," Lizzie suggested.

"I like that. Maybe I can do that without falling. At least it is easier than hopscotch."

"Okay, I'll ask them if that's all right with you."

"Fine with me."

The two girls walked into their classroom. Lizzie went over to Robin to extend the invitation to play with her and Corrie at recess. "Hey, Robin, Corrie and I are going to play a game on the four-square court at recess today. We want you to join us. We thought Wendy would be a good fourth one to join us. Will you play with us?"

"Me play with the twin klutzes? I'm sure it will be hilarious. At least Wendy can make things more even."

Lizzie nodded her partial consent and walked over to Corrie and said, "Well, she said she would, but I don't think she will make it easy for you."

"Oh, that's great. I can just hear Robin now . . ." Corrie's voice trailed off as Mrs. Sipp told them to have a seat. When she had called the class to order, and they had gone through their usual morning routine, Mrs. Sipp said, "Now I would like for you to begin thinking about your science projects that are due in November. You may choose anything from the human body, weather, or outer space. You will need to make a poster and do both a written and oral report. Those are the basics. You may add anything else you like. You will

Fall Doings

work alone, not in groups; however, you may ask me, Mrs. Kegan, or your parents for assistance. I will be giving you a list of requirements along with a grading rubric. Are there any questions?"

Bobby raised his hand and asked, "Can I use a model kit or Legos to build a space capsule?"

"You are not allowed to use pre-made kits, but if you want to design something out of Legos or Tinker Toys, feel free to do so."

Corrie raised her hand and asked, "I have an idea. Can I study a disease and talk about it?"

"That depends. Why don't you and I talk about it privately and you can tell me your idea?"

"Okay. Thank you."

"Are there any other questions?" The class was silent.

"If not, I would like to have your topics by next Monday. Write what you want to do, what you want to learn, and how you plan to go about it."

The rest of the morning quickly passed as they discussed their reading assignments, worked on their maps of Narnia and wrote comparisons of Lucy and Edmund. Soon it was time for recess and free play on the playground. Lizzie ran ahead to claim a four-square court. When Corrie, Wendy, and Robin arrived, they began their game.

At first, things went really well with each girl playing fairly. As the game progressed, Corrie swallowed hard and ventured to speak to Robin. "Robin, may I ask you something?"

Robin responded, rudely, "What?"

"There's this Girls Club at my church. We meet on Friday nights. It's loads of fun. Would you like to come? Wendy can come too if she wants to."

Best Friends and Bullies

Robin burst into laughter as she said, "You're kidding, right? Me go to church? That's the craziest thing I've ever heard."

Then in an attempt to change the subject, she suggested, "Let's pick up the pace. This game is moving too slow." Then she threw the ball really hard – no bounces – to Corrie. She caught it with some effort and sent it on to Wendy. Wendy threw it to Lizzie who returned it to Robin. Robin threw it to Corrie again who was unprepared for the strength of the throw and was thrown off balance by an attempt to catch it. She called out, and Lizzie ran to steady her before she hit the ground. In a wavering voice, Corrie said, "I'm so sorry, but I need to go the classroom and sit down."

As she left, she heard Robin shout, "I just don't know what is wrong with that girl. She can't do anything right. I'll bet she is failing half her classes. Have you seen her handwriting? A kindergarten baby could do better."

Then she heard Lizzie say, "Robin, would you be quiet? She can't help it. One day she might talk about why she has those difficulties, but until then, leave her alone. And by the way, she makes good grades!" Then she stomped off to return to the classroom to check on her friend, leaving Robin and Wendy staring with open mouths.

When Lizzie got back to the classroom, she noticed that Corrie was talking to Mrs. Sipp. Rather than going to them, she got a nod from Mrs. Sipp and went to the reading nook in the back of the classroom.

Meanwhile, Corrie was explaining to Mrs. Sipp what had happened without tattling or blaming anyone. She completed her remarks with a request, "Because I have NF, I would really like to do my science project on it. Maybe the kids in the class will understand my problem a little better."

Fall Doings

Mrs. Sipp looked at her and said, "Corrie, that's a marvelous idea. Do you think you can get the information you need?"

"I think so. Mom is a nurse, and I can get stuff from my doctors. I also have a grown-up friend whose name is Miss Sadie. She has NF and can help me."

"Well, then I would say 'Go for it' and let me know if it becomes too difficult. Now go talk to Lizzie back there. She looks worried."

Corrie and Lizzie sat together in the book nook until the rest of the class came in. They didn't say much; they didn't need to. Corrie quietly, but excitedly shared with Lizzie that she had decided on her science project.

She said, "I just talked to Mrs. Sipp. She said I could do my project on NF since it has to do with the human body. I really hope it will help people like Robin to understand my problems."

Lizzie's eyes lit up with pleasure, "Corrie, that is a great idea. How did you ever think of it?"

"Oh, I don't know. I think I just got really frustrated and thought maybe if people understood, they would be a little nicer to me."

"Well, all I can say is that it's worth a try."

Chapter 17
Lizzie Sleeps Over

As the students entered the classroom from free play, Robin looked over in their direction with a sneer, and quickly returned to her seat. Nothing more was said about the incident on the ball court. The rest of the day passed without event, and soon it was time to go home.

That evening as Corrie's family ate supper, she shared her plans regarding her science project with her parents.

"Mom, can you help me write my proposal for the project after supper? It's not due until next Monday, but it would be nice to get it done."

"Sure, I'll be happy to. I'm glad you're not waiting until the last minute."

That evening, Corrie and her mother sat at the kitchen table and began to answer the questions provided by Mrs. Sipp.

Corrie said, "Now let's see, I have to write a few sentences telling what I want to do, a few sentences telling what I want to learn, and how I plan to go about it."

She started writing:

> I want to do my science project on NF. It's a disease, really a disorder that I have had since I

was a baby, but we just found out about it. I want to learn why I have it and what it may mean in the future. I have a grown-up friend named Miss Sadie, who also has NF. She has to walk with a walker and has lots of pain. I want to help my classmates understand why I am no good at games. I will talk to my doctors, Miss Sadie, and my parents. I will read brochures and other pieces of information. I will also take a picture of the brace I wear on my back. Maybe this will help people understand why I am the way I am."

She stopped writing and asked her mother, "How does this sound?" Her mother took it and read it. After reading it, she said, "I think it sounds just right. Now copy it over in your very best handwriting – take your time."

"Okay, I will."

Corrie copied her work very carefully with no strikeouts. Then she clipped it into her binder and started doing the rest of her homework. It actually went quickly, and she was pleased to have time to read her library book since she had a book report due soon.

Mrs. Sipp approved Corrie's proposal for her project, and Corrie began to work on it. First, she made a list of questions for her doctors. Then she made a list of questions for Miss Sadie. Finally, she made a list of questions for her parents. The weeks quickly passed as fall progressed. The second week in November, Lizzie's parents decided to visit her sister, who was in college. She was in a major dramatic production and wanted her parents to see her. There was also a new boyfriend she wanted them to meet. They asked if Lizzie could stay with the Cushmans. They planned to

Lizzie Sleeps Over

leave on Tuesday and return on Friday. The girls were really excited and began to make plans for their time together. "If only we didn't have to go to school," Lizzie moaned.

"Oh well, we can have fun after school and at night. Maybe we won't have much homework then."

On the Tuesday morning that the Longs were leaving, Mr. Long dropped Lizzie's suitcase off at the Cushman's house and then drove the girls to school. It was very cloudy and unseasonably cold for early November. As Lizzie looked out the car window, she remarked, "I sure wish it would snow."

Mr. Long replied, "I think it's a little early and besides the ground is too warm to allow much to stick even if it did snow."

About that time, he pulled up at the school, and the girls got out of the car. Lizzie turned and gave her father one last kiss as she said, "Bye, Daddy. I love you; see you on Friday."

The girls walked in together. As they chatted, Corrie asked Lizzie, "Aren't you worried about your parents driving all the way to your sister's college?"

"No. We prayed about it this morning. I know God will take care of them."

"I really think it's great that you trust God so much. Maybe someday I will, too."

"You will. The more you learn about Jesus, the more you will trust Him."

By that time, the girls had reached their classroom. The day began with math and a discussion concerning geometric shapes. As the morning progressed, the class grew more restless. Everyone kept glancing outside, hoping to see snow falling from the sky. Mrs. Sipp finally decided to assign a creative writing exercise that they would illustrate after lunch. Each student would describe the most original snowman they could imagine – and then after lunch, they would draw the snowman they described. They had to use as many of the geometric shapes that they had been studying as possible. Before they went home, they would read and discuss a chapter in their novel and have a review for the practice spelling test to be given the next day.

At the beginning of the year, Mrs. Sipp had promised a free afternoon in which students could explore any topic of their choosing . . . if the entire class made 95% or higher on their practice test. So far, they had not yet achieved it, so everyone was hoping it might happen this week.

The class enjoyed the opportunity to express their creativity. By the time the illustrations were done, the classroom was filled with many unusual snowmen. By the end of the day, the clouds thickened, but still, no snow was falling from the sky to the disappointment of Mrs. Sipp and the students. School was dismissed, and the girls walked to Corrie's house where Bessie had hot chocolate and cheese crackers waiting for them. Then they sat down to review their spelling words.

Later that evening, when they were satisfied that they had a firm grasp on the words, the girls turned their attention to recreation. Since both girls liked board games, they chose one from Corrie's extensive collection. They sat down at the kitchen table where they could enjoy the aroma of supper. Corrie had to concede that her mother was right; Bessie cooked the food just the way they liked it. The girls were head to head in their game when they heard Corrie's parents arriving. Together, they moved the game board to a different area of the house and returned to set the table.

As Corrie's parents came in, Dad remarked, "It's brutal out there. It wouldn't surprise me to see some snow in the next day or so. It's not going to get any warmer." Then he turned to Bessie and asked, "Bessie, would you be willing to bring some extra clothes? We might need you to spend the night? I can pick you up to make it easier to carry your paraphernalia."

"I will, and it would be helpful if you would."

"Very well, I will see you at about 7:00 in the morning."

After Bessie left, the Cushmans and Lizzie enjoyed supper together. The girls helped clean the kitchen. After that, Mrs. Cushman assisted in a spelling review in which both girls proved that they were definitely ready to do well in the upcoming practice test.

After the review they finished the game they had started before supper with Corrie winning; however, it really didn't matter who won. The girls just enjoyed being together. Soon it was time for bed, and the girls managed to get ready in time to read for a few minutes.

By the next morning, the clouds had thickened, and the temperature had dropped outside. The girls wore heavy winter coats as they made their way to school. They were both thankful that the walk was short and that the school building was warm. As they took their seats in the classroom, they glanced outside, hoping that they might see a flake or two falling from the sky. When the bell rang, Mrs. Sipp called the class to order, with the words, "I know you are excited about the snow we are likely to get, but we have a lot to do today. First, let's get the practice spelling test out of the way. Take about five minutes to review and to get your minds in gear." When the five minutes were up, she instructed, "Okay, clear your desks, and take out a clean sheet of paper."

When the test had been given and the papers graded, they discovered that everyone had finally achieved the 95% or higher mark. Their cheering was matched by the cheering that came when they looked outside and saw that there was snow falling from the sky. Mrs. Sipp quickly reined the class back in and led them to the library for their weekly visit. They had been instructed to find the material needed for their science projects and to find at least one book for recreational reading since the next day was a teacher workday, and there was no school. Lizzie and Corrie chose their books quickly and sat down at a table.

When the students returned to the classroom, there was an announcement over the loudspeaker that school was being dismissed. Everyone quickly gathered their belongings. Concerned parents were lining up in their cars outside of the building. Students who were walking were dismissed. As they came to the front of the school building, they were surprised but happy to see Bessie standing there with a huge umbrella. The three of them made their way home together. Corrie was especially glad to have Bessie with them since the sidewalks were getting slippery.

It was a relief to all of them that they arrived home safely. The girls took some time to warm up and then sat down to grilled cheese sandwiches and hot chocolate. As they watched the snowfall, Corrie's face showed more and more worry.

Bessie noticed and said, "What's the matter, Corrie?"

Lizzie Sleeps Over

"What if it gets so deep that Mom and Daddy can't get home, or they have a wreck on the way home?"

"Have you prayed and asked the Lord to keep them safe?"

"No. I guess I should."

Lizzie chimed in, "Yes, we should. Can we pray for my parents too?"

The three of them prayed together. Then Bessie invited the two girls to help her make supper – meatloaf and baked potatoes. She helped Corrie mix up the meatloaf and put it in a pan. Then they put it in the refrigerator to rest for a while. Lizzie scrubbed the potatoes and wrapped them in foil. They would open a can of green peas just before supper.

Then the girls settled down to a rematch of the game they had been playing the night before. The game lasted throughout the afternoon with each girl winning several times. Soon the smell of meatloaf and potatoes wafted through the house. Just before 5:00, Corrie heard the familiar sound of her parents' car in the carport. She ran to the door to greet them. They had been allowed to leave work early and had made their way home braving the snow-covered road.

Corrie and Lizzie helped Bessie put supper on the table. As soon as her parents had changed into more comfortable clothes, they all sat down to supper.

They talked a lot about the snowstorm, and Lizzie expressed her concern for her parent's safety, but she was reassured when the Cushmans told her they had been following the weather patterns and that it was likely all rain where her parents were visiting, and the snow would probably be gone by the time they got home. It had stopped snowing by the time the girls went to bed, but they dutifully took their books with them and read for a while.

The next morning, the girls slept in but did their reading after breakfast. Corrie also completed her science project. After lunch, the girls offered to help Bessie make beef stew for supper. She was making an extra-large portion so that the leftovers could be turned into vegetable soup, which would welcome the Longs home the following evening. The girls begged Bessie to let them make dessert. They were all pleased with the results – chocolate sheet cake.

The rest of the day passed with another game marathon. Neither girl ventured outside, Corrie for fear of falling and Lizzie out of deference for Corrie.

The next day was considerably warmer, and the snowy mess began to leave. Both girls made a concentrated effort to complete the required reading, before one final marathon of board games. Soon it was time for Corrie's parents to arrive from work. As soon as they got home, Mr. Cushman took Bessie home. While he was gone, Lizzie's parents returned from their trip. When Mr. Cushman arrived back home, they all sat down to a meal of homemade vegetable soup and homemade fried apple pies. The Longs left shortly after supper, and the Cushmans resumed their regular Friday night activities. Corrie asked her parents if she could practice her report on them, and they gladly consented.

Corrie stood before her parents with her poster in hand, took a deep breath, and began. She continued through the entire presentation without stopping. When she was finished, she looked at them and asked, "Well, how did it sound?"

Lizzie Sleeps Over

Her mother replied, "I thought it sounded just right, but you need to slow down. You're not in a marathon to finish as fast as you can."

Corrie nodded as her father added, "You know we're so proud of you. This is a big step for you. Why don't we pray together that the Lord would bless your efforts and use this to His glory?"

Corrie and her parents joined hands and prayed. Then Corrie went to bed basking in the pleasure of her parents' approval. They all knew that God would bless Corrie's efforts.

Chapter 18
Corrie's Science Project

On Monday morning, she stood before her classmates and teacher. She took a deep breath and began.

"My science project is pretty personal. Most of you know that I am really clumsy and don't play sports very well. I know some of you call me Clumsy Corrie, and while that really hurts my feelings, it's all right. I understand why I'm that way, but most of you don't. I have a neurological disorder called NF. NF is what they call a genetic disorder —that means it's not contagious even though you see a lot of bumps when you look at me. My science project is called 'My NF Road.'

When I was little, I had trouble with my legs and hips. I had to wear a brace to help me walk right. I remember asking my Mom, "Do I really have to wear it?" She always said, "Yes," and so I wore it. My parents thought that something really must be wrong when they saw these funny brown patches and odd bumps on my body. We went to lots of doctors, and finally one of them said he thought I had NF. He told me that the funny bumps were neurofibromas and that the brown patches were café au lait spots – that means coffee with cream.

Best Friends and Bullies

I know my head is bigger than most other kids' because regular hats don't fit me. I also know that people like to make fun of that because last year a boy in another class called me the kid with the stretched head. One thing I'm really thankful for is that I don't have severe learning disabilities that some people with NF have.

I have always walked funny and can't do things with my hands. My doctor says that I am uncoordinated and it's just a part of having NF. That's why I don't run or play ball games very well. Some people with NF have a curved spine – I do, too. I have to wear a brace to help strengthen weak muscles. I named him Goofball because he is goofing up my life.

Sometimes as people get older, NF causes problems. I have a grown-up friend, whose name is Miss Sadie. She is pretty old; I think she is around 50. Like me, she has NF and found out about it when she was little. She has terrible balance and walks with a walker named Ebenezer. She says the name Ebenezer is from the Bible and said that the name means 'stone of help,' and it reminds her that the Lord is with her no matter what. She has hydrocephalus, which means there is too much fluid in her head. So, she has shunt to help drain it. She still gets lots of headaches and has other pain. One thing she told me is that she refuses to allow NF to define who she is. She says she is a child of God and that He knew she would be born with NF, but that He can use her pain and weakness to make Him look great and that's all that matters. I don't know what will happen with my NF as I get older. Like Miss Sadie, I may need a shunt or a walker. I only know one thing. Jesus is my Savior, and He will help me walk my NF Road."

Connie's Science Project

The class applauded as Corrie sat down. Lizzie looked over and gave her a thumbs-up, but the best thing that happened that day was at lunch. Robin walked over to the table where Corrie and Lizzie were sitting and asked, "May I sit with you?"

Both girls shrugged and motioned toward an empty chair where Robin sat down. Robin looked at Corrie and said, "You're different. You never get mad at me when I make fun of you. You're not even mad at God because of the NF. I know I laughed at you when you invited me to that Girls Club at your church, but now I think I would like to go. I want to meet that Miss Sadie and see if God can make a difference in my life, too. May I go with you?"

Neither girl hesitated as they answered, "Yes!"

Later that afternoon, as they were walking home, Corrie said to Lizzie, "You know, it really does pay to live for God and trust Him in the hard times, doesn't it?"

About the Author

Dr. Catherine Chatmon was born in Winston-Salem and is a lifelong resident of the city. She wrote her first story when she was seven years old and continued to develop her skill under the tutelage and encouragement of her parents and various teachers.

Upon graduation from high school, she enrolled at what was then Piedmont Bible College and graduated with a BA in Bible/Christian Education. Desiring to serve the Lord as an educator for missionary children, she enrolled at UNC-G. Here she pursued a degree in Library Science with a view toward school librarianship, but God had other plans.

Several roadblocks, particularly those related to her neurofibromatosis and its residual effects, redirected her to the field of higher education. Since 1984, she has had the joy of serving the Lord at Piedmont International University in both the Library and in the Moore School of Education. During this time, she has earned a second master's in religious education and fulfilled her dream of earning a doctorate in Education from Regent University,

With the publication of *Best Friends and Bullies*, another life-long dream has come to fruition.